SMURFS
THE VILLAGE BEHIND THE WALL

Peyo

the SMURFS™

THE VILLAGE BEHIND THE WALL

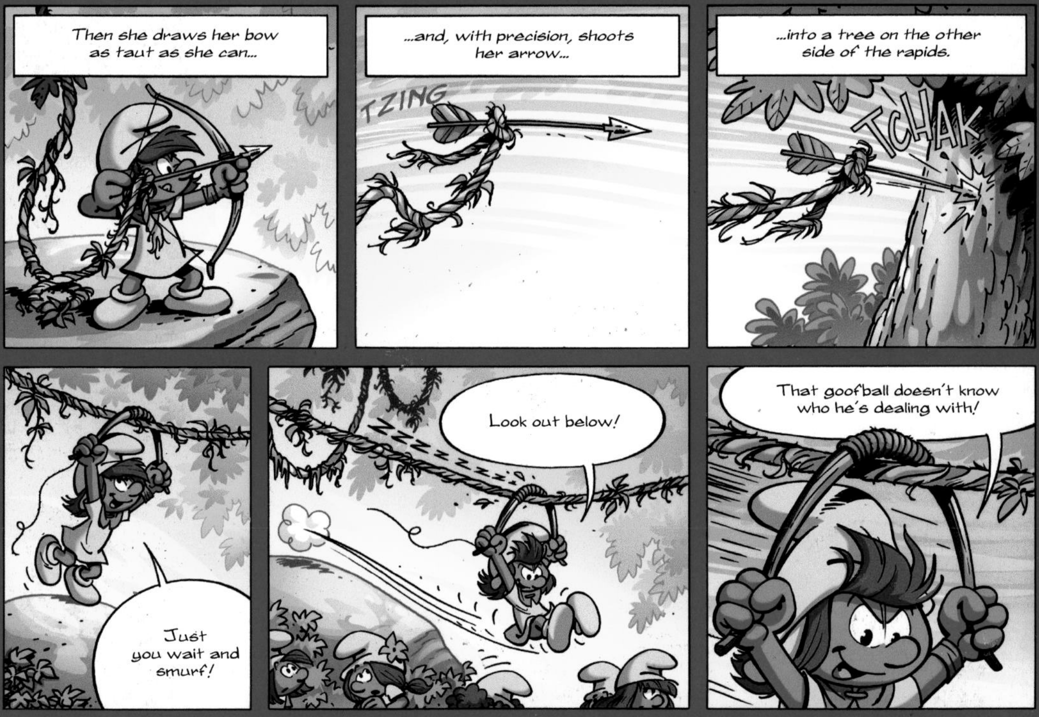

Then she draws her bow as taut as she can...
...and, with precision, shoots her arrow...
TZING
...into a tree on the other side of the rapids.
TCHAK
Just you wait and smurf!
Look out below!
That goofball doesn't know who he's dealing with!

A SMURFS GRAPHIC NOVEL BY PEYO

WITH THE COLLABORATION OF
LUC PARTHOENS AND ALAIN JOST – SCRIPT
ALAIN MAURY, JEROEN DE CONINCK, MIGUEL DIAZ AND LAURENT CAGNIAT – ART
PAOLO MADDELENI – COLOR

PAPERCUTZ™
NEW YORK

SMURFS GRAPHIC NOVELS AVAILABLE FROM PAPERCUTZ™

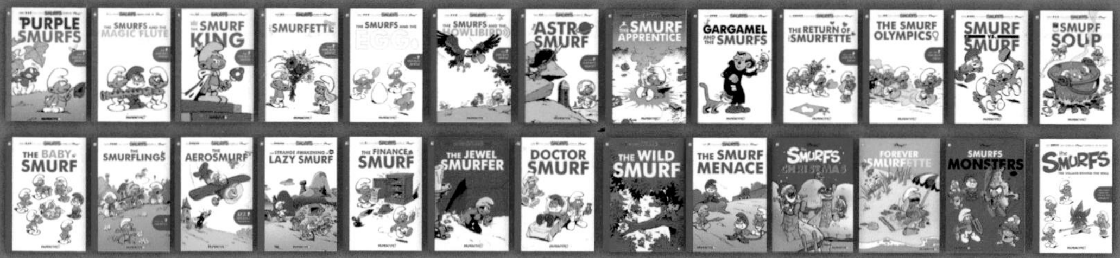
PURPLE SMURFS
THE SMURFS AND THE MAGIC FLUTE
THE SMURF KING
SMURFETTE
THE SMURFS AND THE EGG
THE SMURFS AND THE HOWLIBIRD
ASTRO SMURF
THE SMURF APPRENTICE
GARGAMEL AND THE SMURFS
THE RETURN OF THE SMURFETTE
THE SMURF OLYMPICS
SMURF VS. SMURF
SMURF SOUP
THE BABY SMURF
SMURFLINGS
AEROSMURF
THE STRANGE AWAKENING OF LAZY SMURF
THE FINANCE SMURF
THE JEWEL SMURFER
DOCTOR SMURF
THE WILD SMURF
THE SMURF MENACE
SMURFS CHRISTMAS
FOREVER SMURFETTE
SMURFS MONSTERS
THE SMURFS

1. **THE PURPLE SMURFS**
2. **THE SMURFS AND THE MAGIC FLUTE**
3. **THE SMURF KING**
4. **THE SMURFETTE**
5. **THE SMURFS AND THE EGG**
6. **THE SMURFS AND THE HOWLIBIRD**
7. **THE ASTROSMURF**
8. **THE SMURF APPRENTICE**
9. **GARGAMEL AND THE SMURFS**
10. **THE RETURN OF THE SMURFETTE**
11. **THE SMURF OLYMPICS**
12. **SMURF VS. SMURF**
13. **SMURF SOUP**
14. **THE BABY SMURF**
15. **THE SMURFLINGS**
16. **THE AEROSMURF**
17. **THE STRANGE AWAKENING OF LAZY SMURF**
18. **THE FINANCE SMURF**
19. **THE JEWEL SMURFER**
20. **DOCTOR SMURF**
21. **THE WILD SMURF**
22. **THE SMURF MENACE**

- **THE SMURF CHRISTMAS**
- **FOREVER SMURFETTE**
- **SMURFS MONSTERS**
- **THE VILLAGE BEHIND THE WALL**

THE SMURFS graphic novels are available in paperback for $5.99 each and in hardcover for $10.99 each, except for THE SMURFS #21,THE SMURFS #22, and THE VILLAGE BEHIND THE WALL which are $7.99 each in paperback and $12.99 each in hardcover, at booksellers everywhere. You can also order online at papercutz.com. Or call 1-800-886-1223, Monday through Friday, 9 – 5 EST. MC, Visa, and AmEx accepted. To order by mail, please add $4.00 for postage and handling for first book ordered, $1.00 for each additional book and make check payable to NBM Publishing. Send to: Papercutz, 160 Broadway, Suite 700, East Wing, New York, NY 10038.

THE SMURFS graphic novels are also available digitally wherever e-books are sold.

PAPERCUTZ.COM

SMURFS THE VILLAGE BEHIND THE WALL

"Brainy Smurf's Walk"
BY PEYO
WITH THE COLLABORATION OF
ALAIN JOST FOR THE SCRIPT,
JEROEN DE CONINCK FOR ARTWORK,
PAOLO MADDELENI FOR COLOR.

"Challenges for Hefty Smurf"
BY PEYO
LUC PARTHOENS FOR THE SCRIPT,
ALAIN MAURY FOR ARTWORK,
PAOLO MADDELENI FOR COLOR.

"Clumsy Smurf's Dragonfly"
BY PEYO
LUC PARTHOENS FOR THE SCRIPT,
LAURENT CAGNIAT FOR ARTWORK,
PAOLO MADDELENI FOR COLOR.

"The Squash Smurfs"
BY PEYO
LUC PARTHOENS FOR THE SCRIPT,
ALAIN MAURY FOR ARTWORK,
PAOLO MADDELENI FOR COLOR.

"Smurflily Strange World"
BY PEYO
WITH THE COLLABORATION OF
ALAIN JOST FOR THE SCRIPT,
MIGUEL DIAZ FOR ARTWORK,
PAOLO MADDELENI FOR COLOR.

Joe Johnson, *SMURFLATIONS*
Adam Grano, *SMURFIC DESIGN*
Janice Chiang, *LETTERING SMURFETTE*
Calvin Louie, *LETTERING ASSISTANT SMURF*
Matt. Murray, *SMURF CONSULTANT*
Sasha Kimiatek, *SMURF COORDINATOR*
Jeff Whitman, *ASSISTANT MANAGING SMURF*
Jim Salicrup, *SMURF-IN-CHIEF*

PAPERBACK EDITION ISBN: 978-1-62991-782-5
HARDCOVER EDITION ISBN: 978-1-62991-783-2

PRINTED IN CHINA MARCH 2017 BY WKT CO. LTD.

Papercutz books may be purchased for business or promotional use. For information on bulk purchases please contact Macmillan Corporate and Premium Sales Department at (800) 221-7945 x5442.

DISTRIBUTED BY MACMILLAN
FIRST PAPERCUTZ PRINTING

MEET THE SMURFS OF SMURFY GROVE

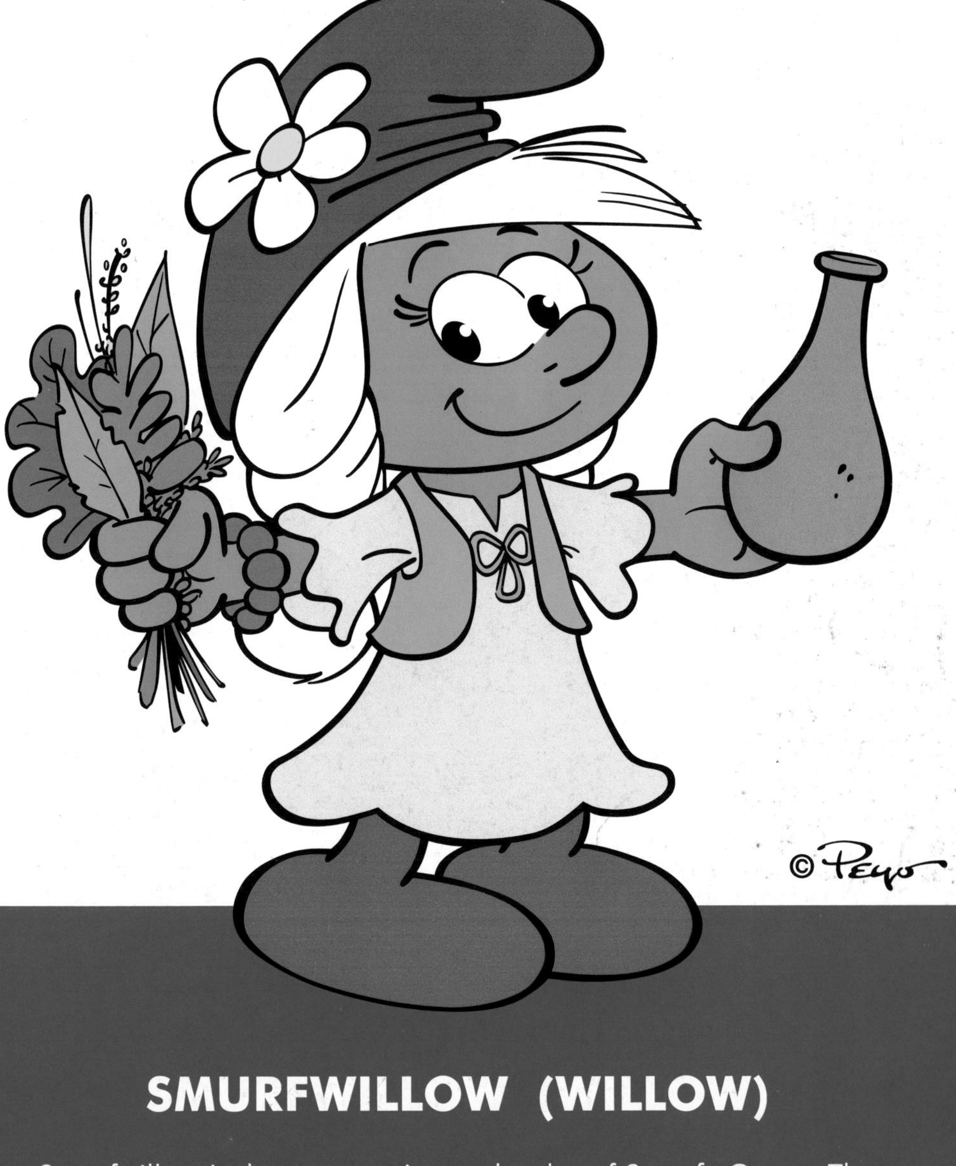
© Peyo

SMURFWILLOW (WILLOW)

Smurfwillow is the magnanimous leader of Smurfy Grove. The decision-maker of the group, Willow has raised her girls to be tough warriors, ready for whatever dangers they may face in the forest. She also has great knowledge of plants and botany, mixing flowers into potions to create healing elixirs.

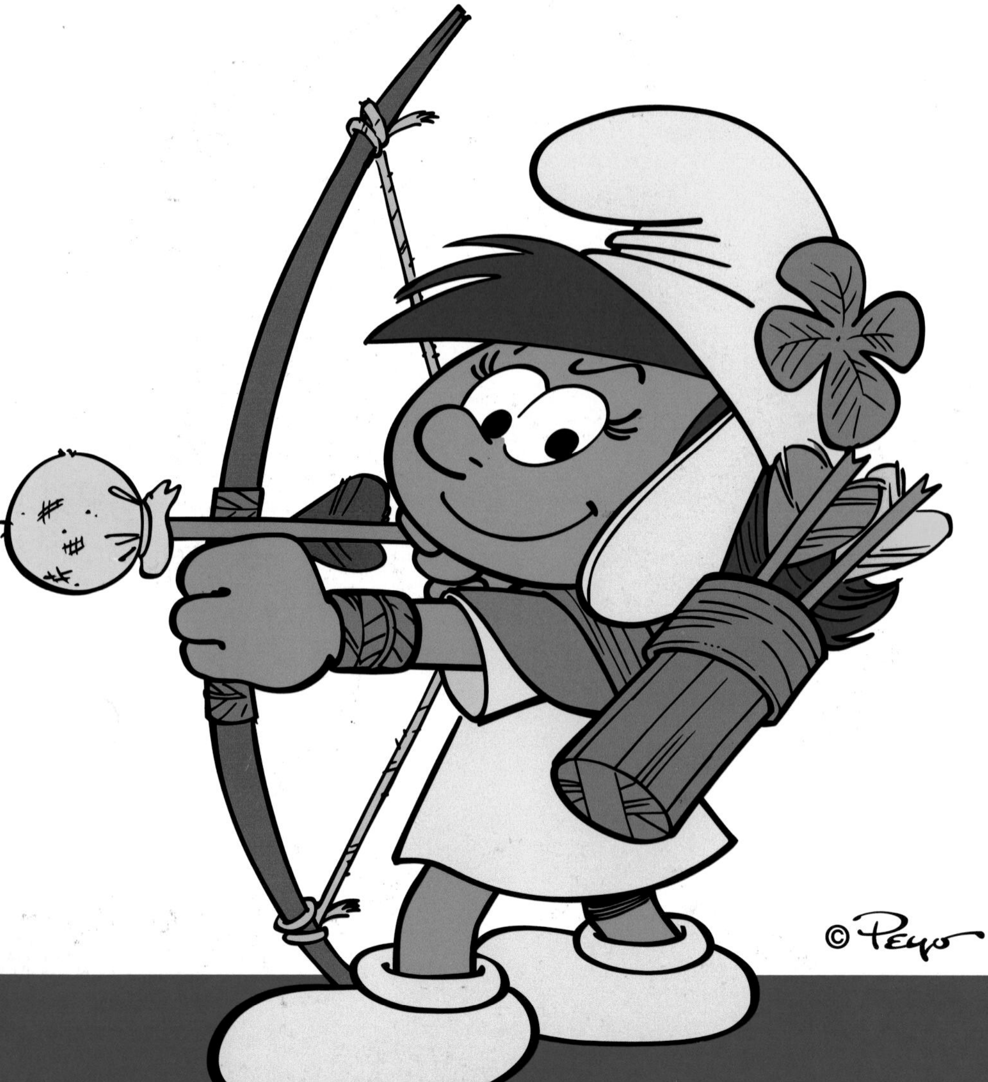
© Peyo

SMURFSTORM (STORMY)

Smurfy Grove is protected thanks to their toughest warrior, Smurfstorm. Good with a bow and arrow and quick to jump into any problem, Smurfstorm is fierce...and fiercely loyal to her friends.

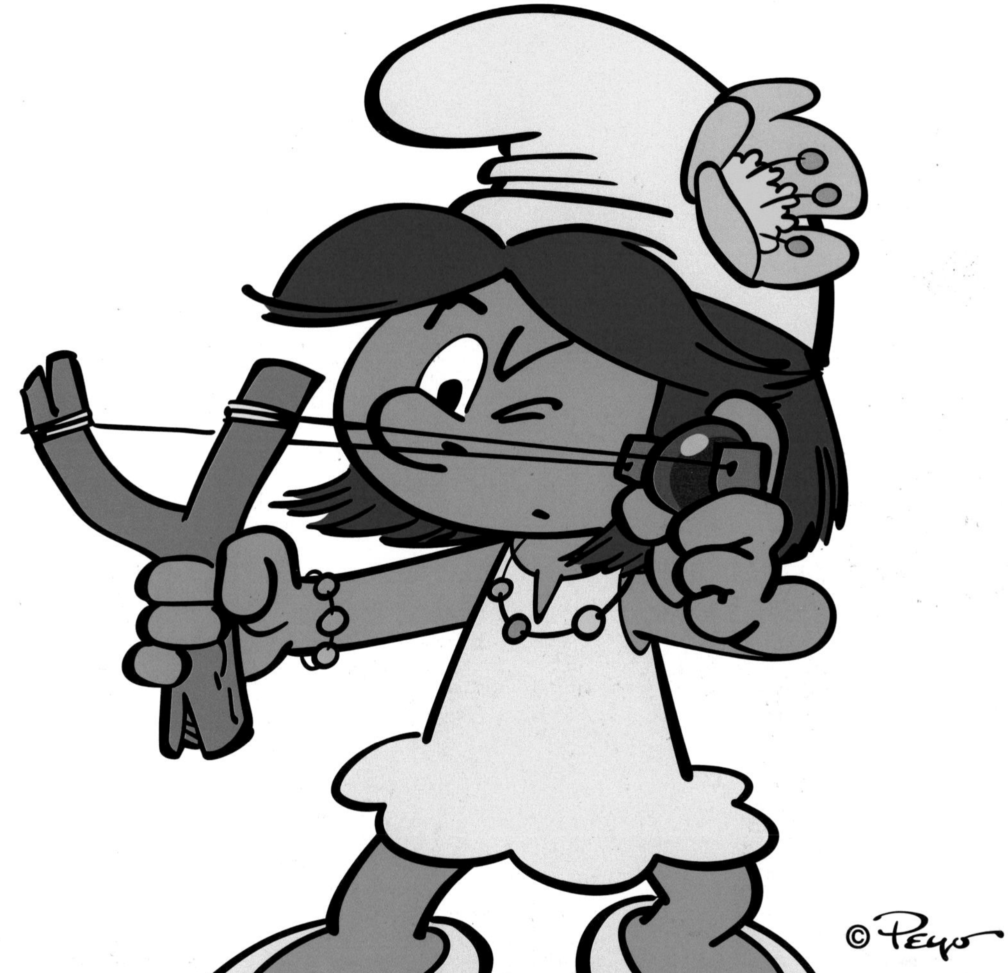
© Peyo

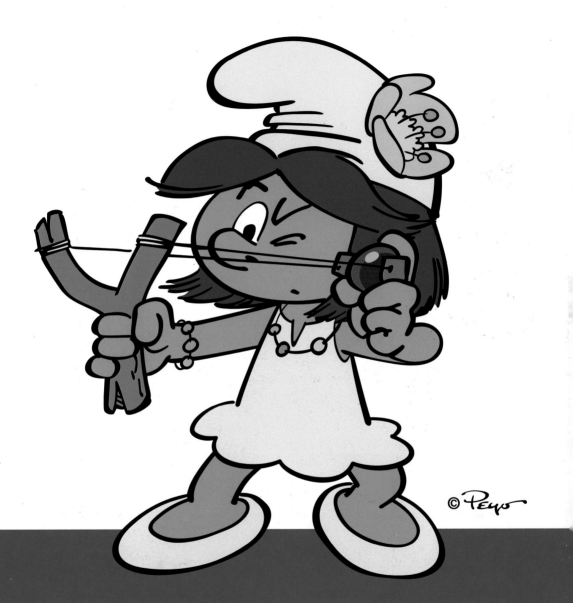

SMURFBLOSSOM (BLOSSOM)

Smurfblossom loves to talk. She can talk about anything to anyone and just talk and talk and talk. Granted with the gift of gab, Blossom can always see the positive side to any situation.

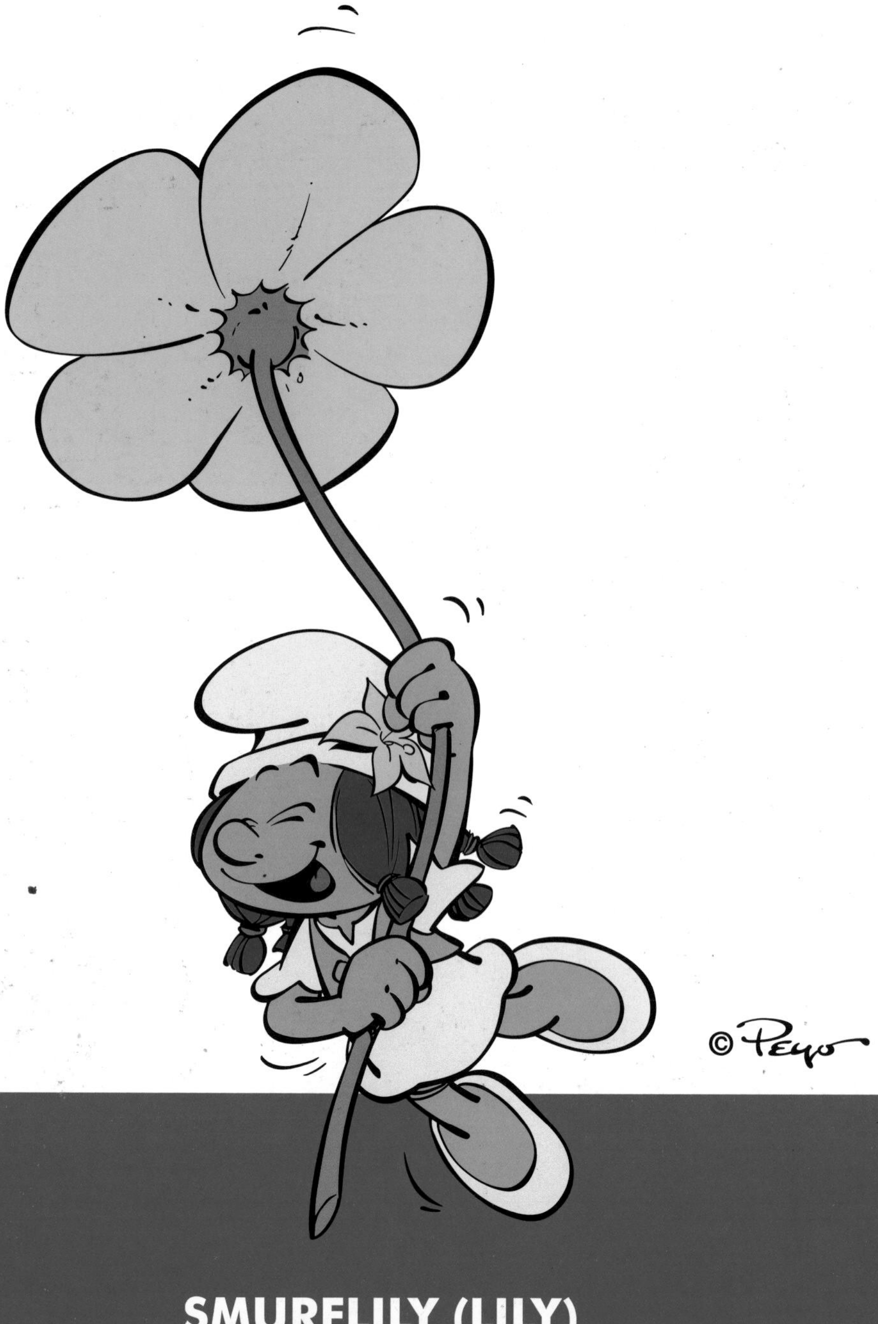
© Peyo

SMURFLILY (LILY)

Smurflily is smart, sassy, and practical. She can be outspoken and at times disagrees with the rest of Smurfy Grove, but she always wants what is best for her sisters.

BRAINY SMURF'S WALK

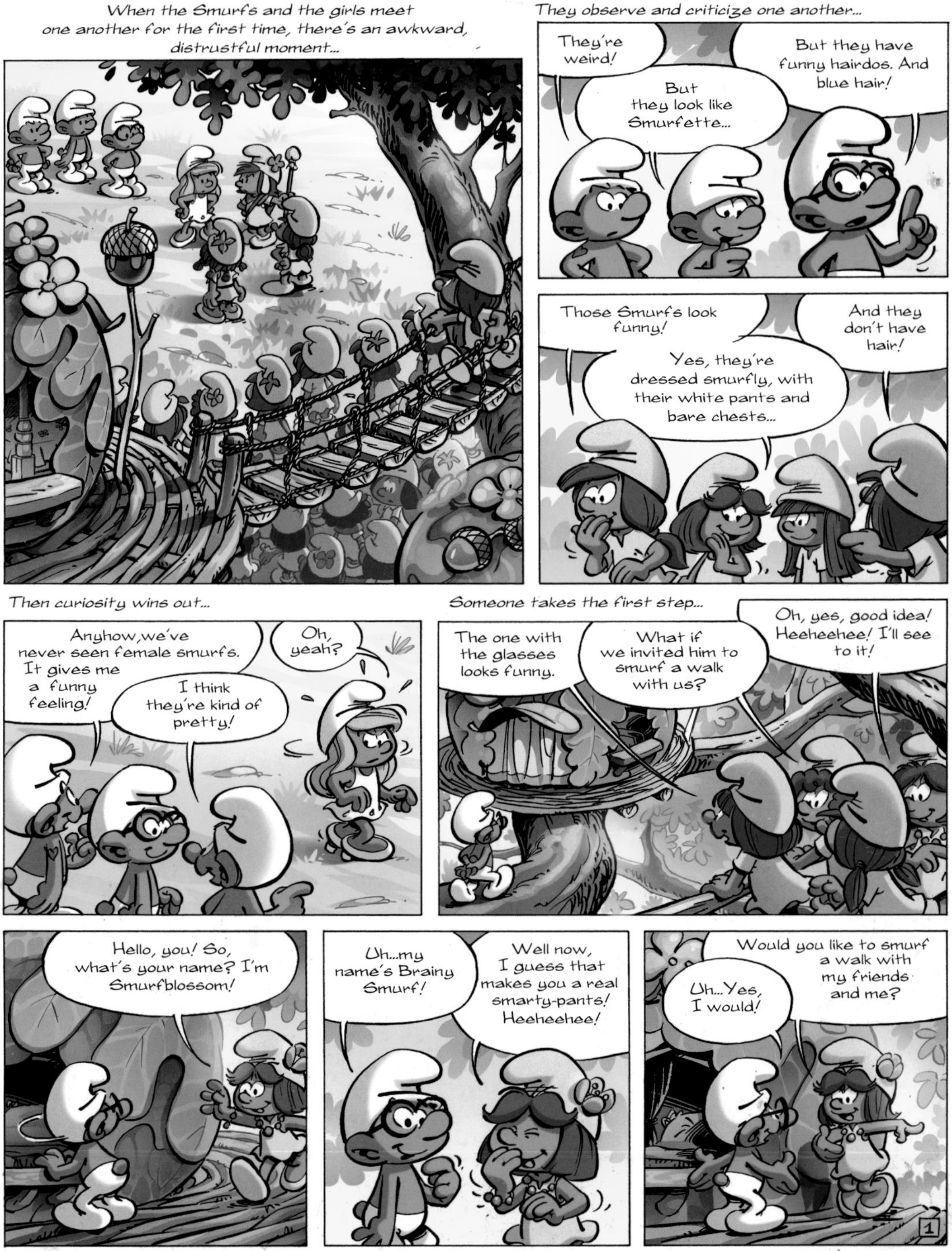

When the Smurfs and the girls meet one another for the first time, there's an awkward, distrustful moment...
They observe and criticize one another...
They're weird!
But they look like Smurfette...
But they have funny hairdos. And blue hair!
Those Smurfs look funny!
Yes, they're dressed smurfly, with their white pants and bare chests...
And they don't have hair!
Then curiosity wins out...
Anyhow, we've never seen female smurfs. It gives me a funny feeling!
I think they're kind of pretty!
Oh, yeah?
Someone takes the first step...
The one with the glasses looks funny.
What if we invited him to smurf a walk with us?
Oh, yes, good idea! Heeheehee! I'll see to it!
Hello, you! So, what's your name? I'm Smurfblossom!
Uh...my name's Brainy Smurf!
Well now, I guess that makes you a real smarty-pants! Heeheehee!
Would you like to smurf a walk with my friends and me?
Uh...Yes, I would!
1

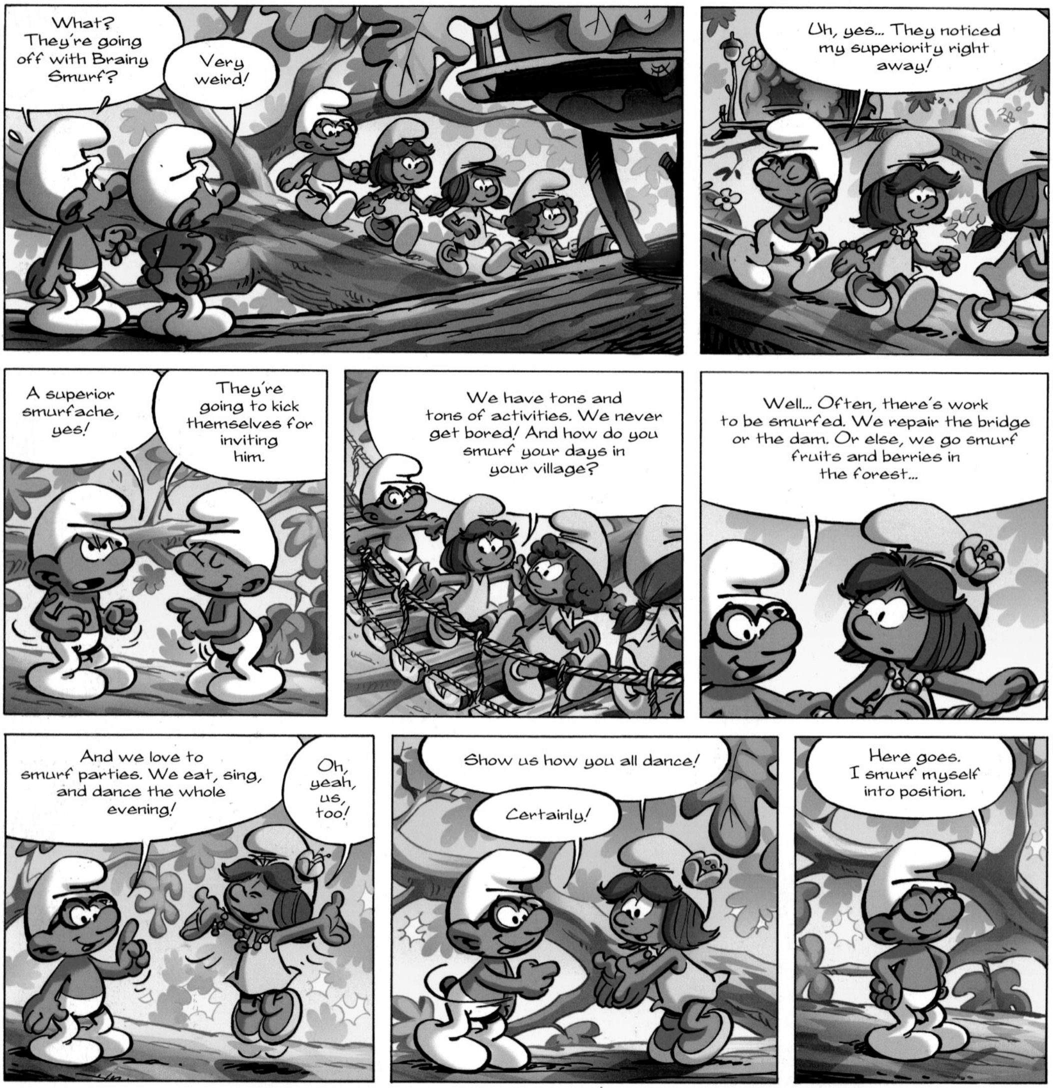

What? They're going off with Brainy Smurf?
Very weird!
Uh, yes... They noticed my superiority right away!
A superior smurfache, yes!
They're going to kick themselves for inviting him.
We have tons and tons of activities. We never get bored! And how do you smurf your days in your village?
Well... Often, there's work to be smurfed. We repair the bridge or the dam. Or else, we go smurf fruits and berries in the forest...
And we love to smurf parties. We eat, sing, and dance the whole evening!
Oh, yeah, us, too!
Show us how you all dance!
Certainly!
Here goes. I smurf myself into position.
Tralalaaa smurflala...
Tralalaaa...
Smurf-lalaaaaa!
Ah, okay... Not terrible!
2

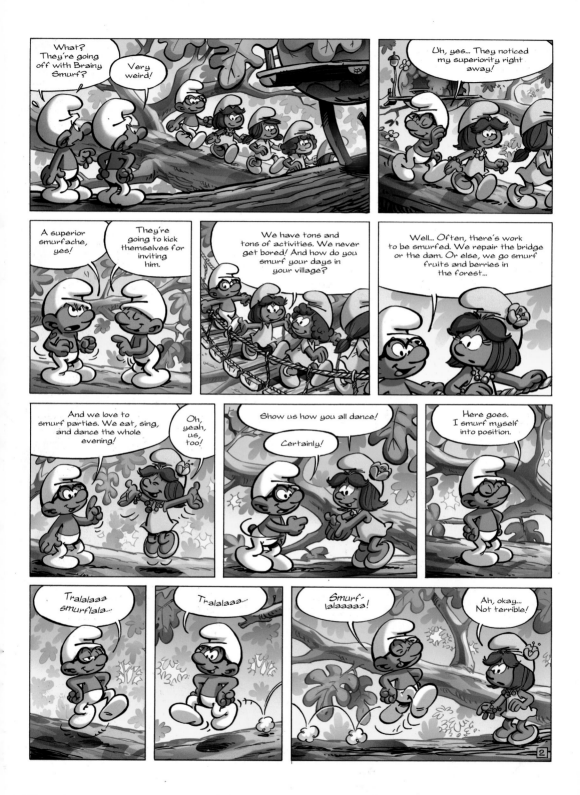

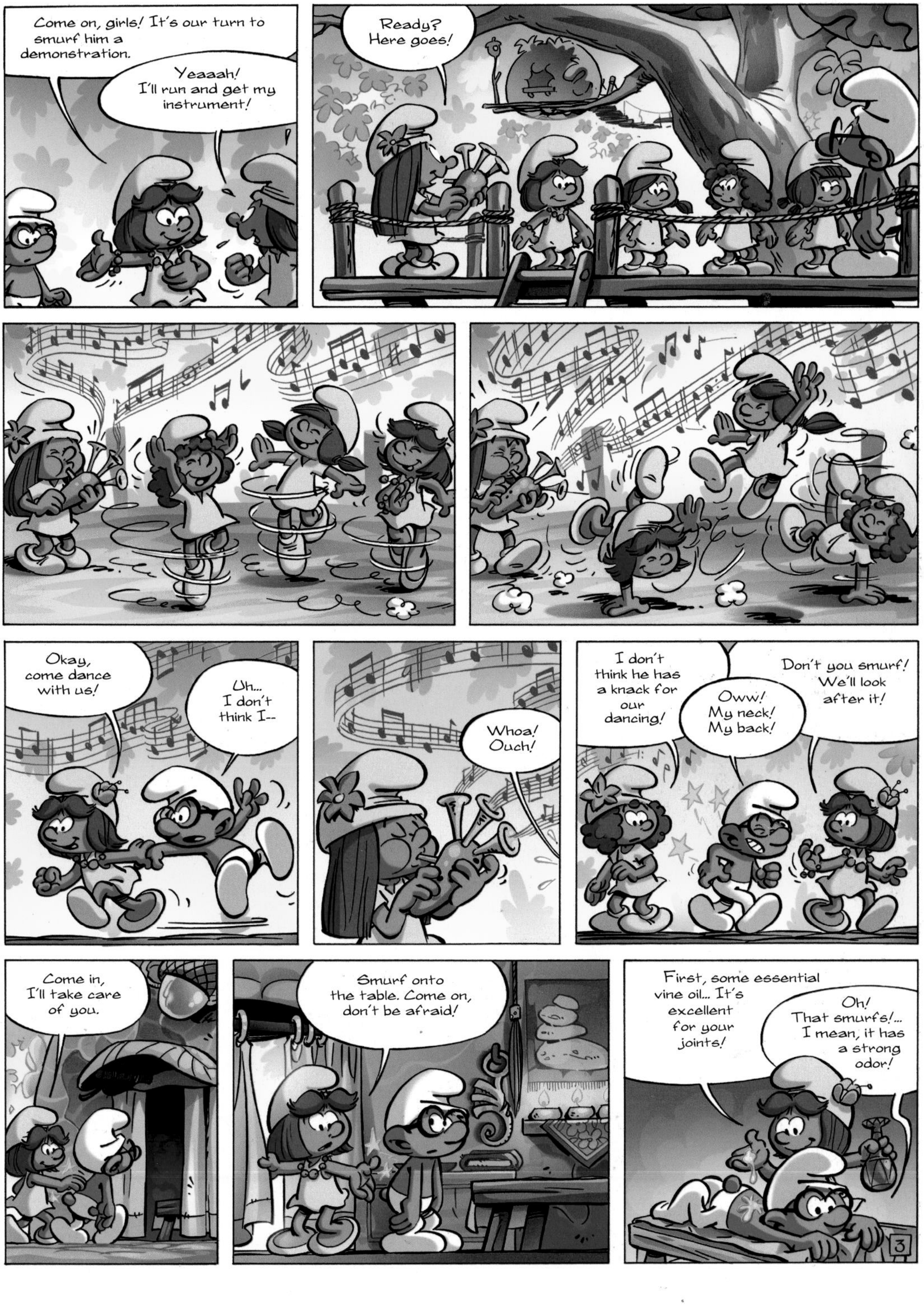
Come on, girls! It's our turn to smurf him a demonstration.
Yeaaah! I'll run and get my instrument!
Ready? Here goes!
Okay, come dance with us!
Uh... I don't think I--
Whoa! Ouch!
I don't think he has a knack for our dancing!
Oww! My neck! My back!
Don't you smurf! We'll look after it!
Come in, I'll take care of you.
Smurf onto the table. Come on, don't be afraid!
First, some essential vine oil... It's excellent for your joints!
Oh! That smurfs!... I mean, it has a strong odor!
3

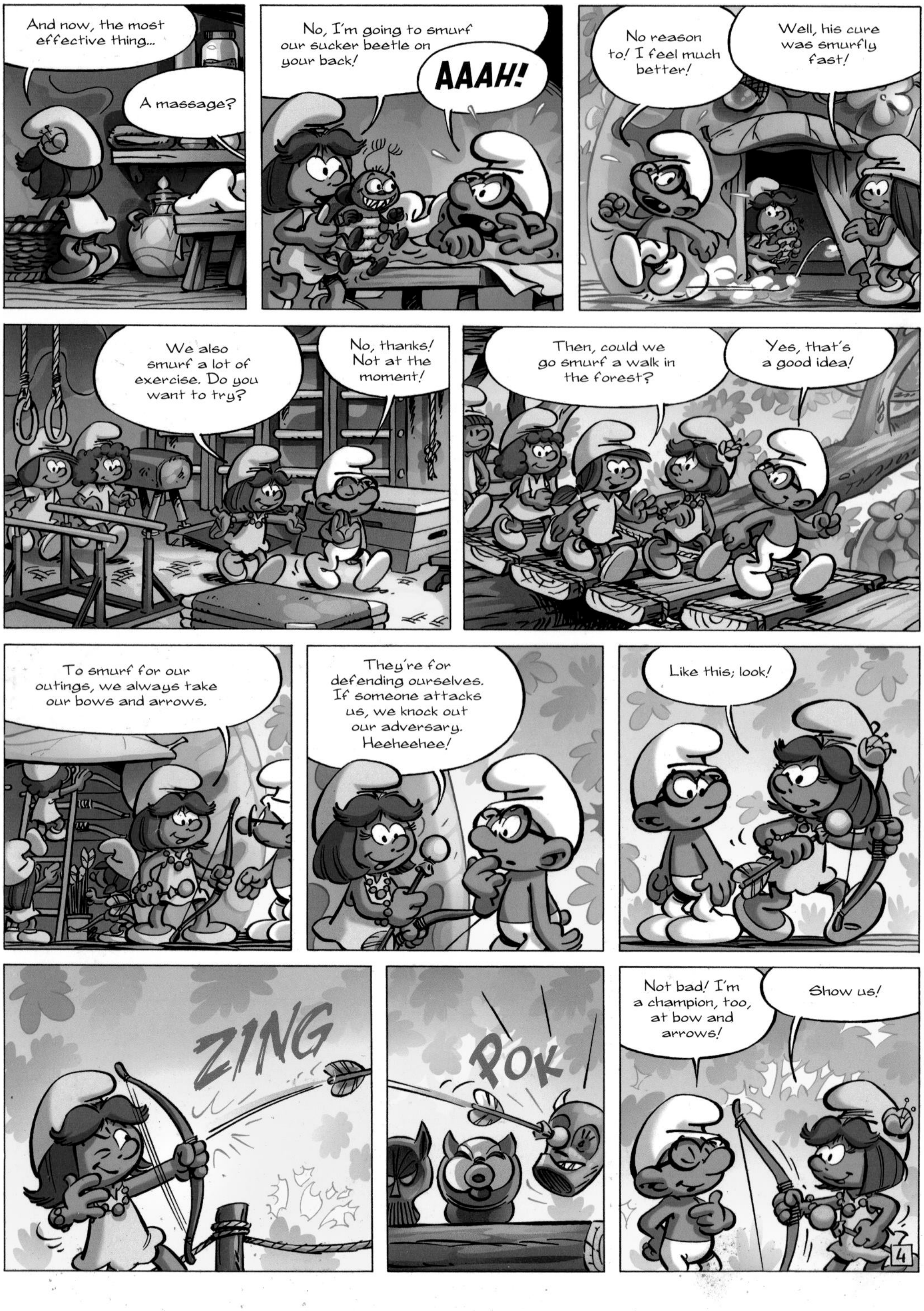
And now, the most effective thing...
A massage?
No, I'm going to smurf our sucker beetle on your back!
AAAH!
No reason to! I feel much better!
Well, his cure was smurfly fast!
We also smurf a lot of exercise. Do you want to try?
No, thanks! Not at the moment!
Then, could we go smurf a walk in the forest?
Yes, that's a good idea!
To smurf for our outings, we always take our bows and arrows.
They're for defending ourselves. If someone attacks us, we knock out our adversary. Heeheehee!
Like this; look!
ZING
POK
Not bad! I'm a champion, too, at bow and arrows!
Show us!
4

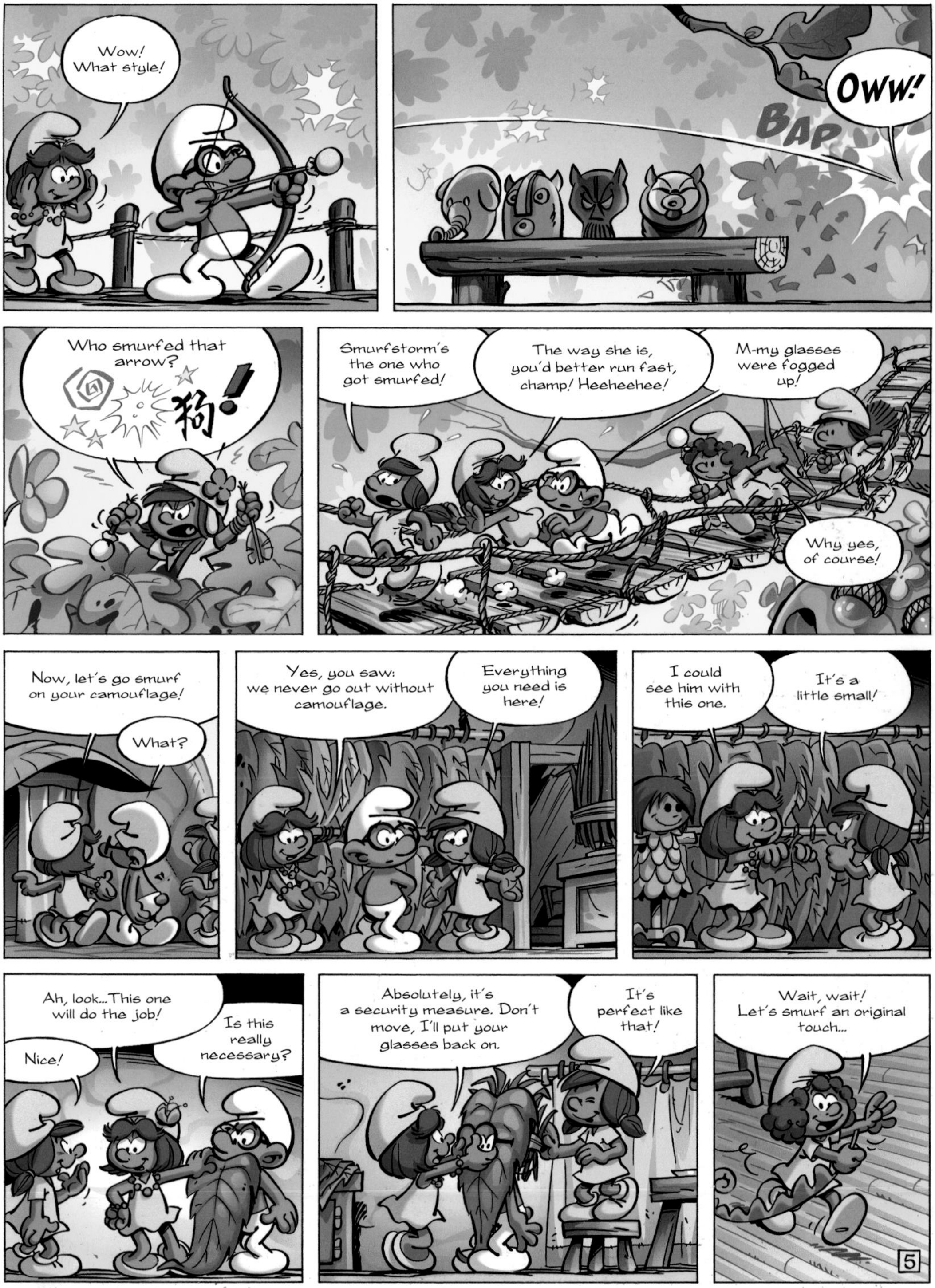
Wow! What style!
OWW!
BAP
Who smurfed that arrow?
Smurfstorm's the one who got smurfed!
The way she is, you'd better run fast, champ! Heeheehee!
M-my glasses were fogged up!
Why yes, of course!
Now, let's go smurf on your camouflage!
What?
Yes, you saw: we never go out without camouflage.
Everything you need is here!
I could see him with this one.
It's a little small!
Ah, look... This one will do the job!
Nice!
Is this really necessary?
Absolutely, it's a security measure. Don't move, I'll put your glasses back on.
It's perfect like that!
Wait, wait! Let's smurf an original touch...
5

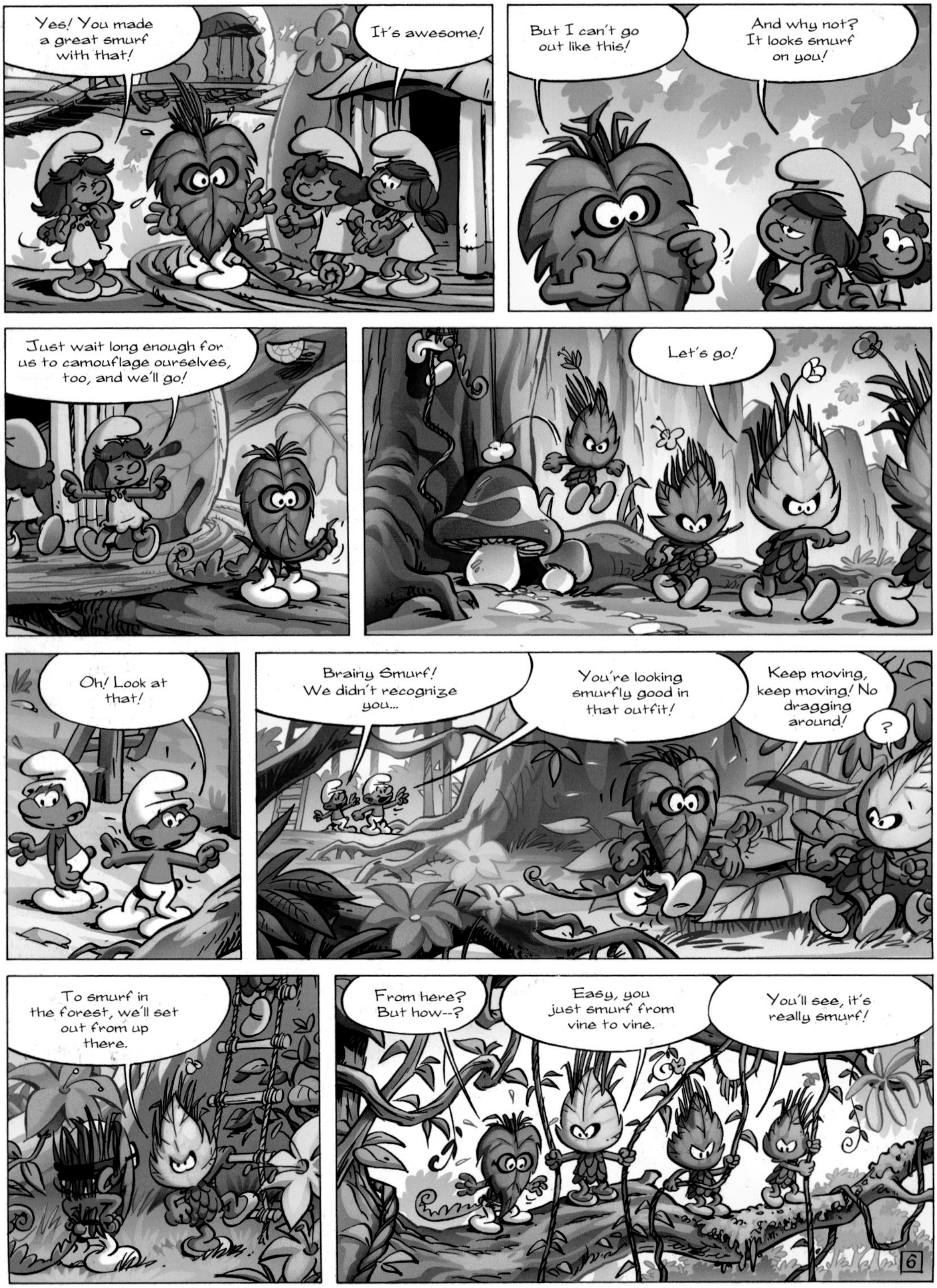
Yes! You made a great smurf with that!
It's awesome!
But I can't go out like this!
And why not? It looks smurf on you!
Just wait long enough for us to camouflage ourselves, too, and we'll go!
Let's go!
Oh! Look at that!
Brainy Smurf! We didn't recognize you...
You're looking smurfly good in that outfit!
Keep moving, keep moving! No dragging around!
?
To smurf in the forest, we'll set out from up there.
From here? But how--?
Easy, you just smurf from vine to vine.
You'll see, it's really smurf!
6

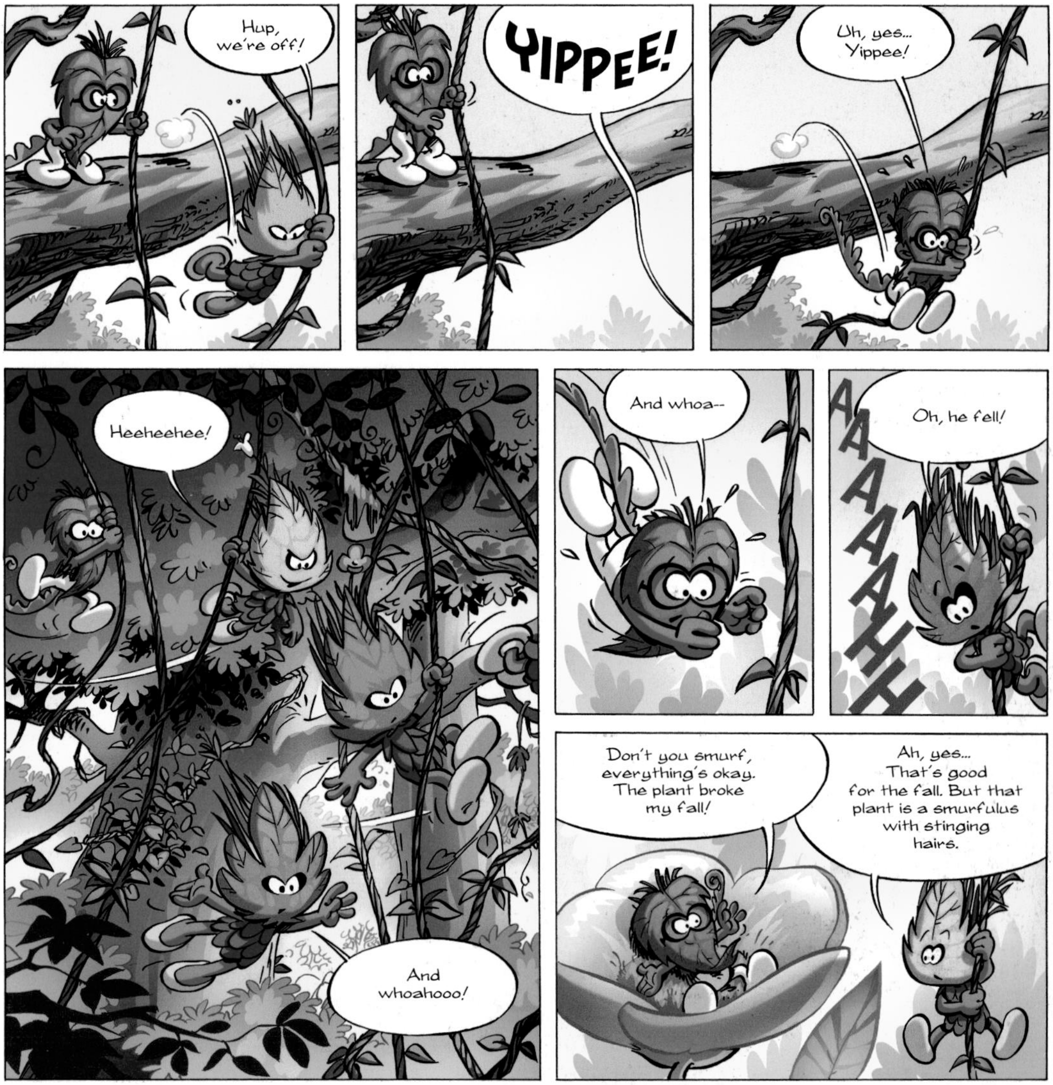

Hup, we're off!
YIPPEE!
Uh, yes... Yippee!
Heeheehee!
And whoahooo!
And whoa--
AAAAAAHH
Oh, he fell!
Don't you smurf, everything's okay. The plant broke my fall!
Ah, yes... That's good for the fall. But that plant is a smurfulus with stinging hairs.
A WHAT?
Yikes! Oww! It burns! Smurf me out of here!
We're coming!
You're better off on solid ground!
7

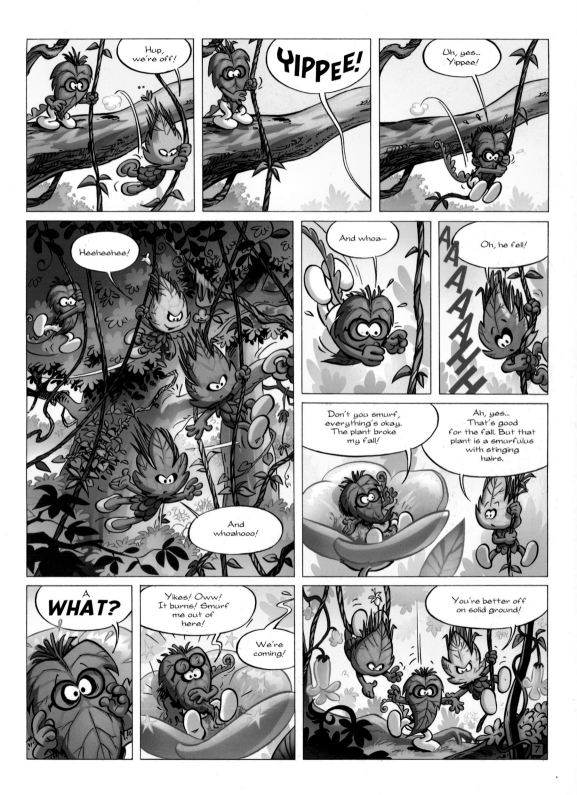

CHALLENGES FOR HEFTY SMURF

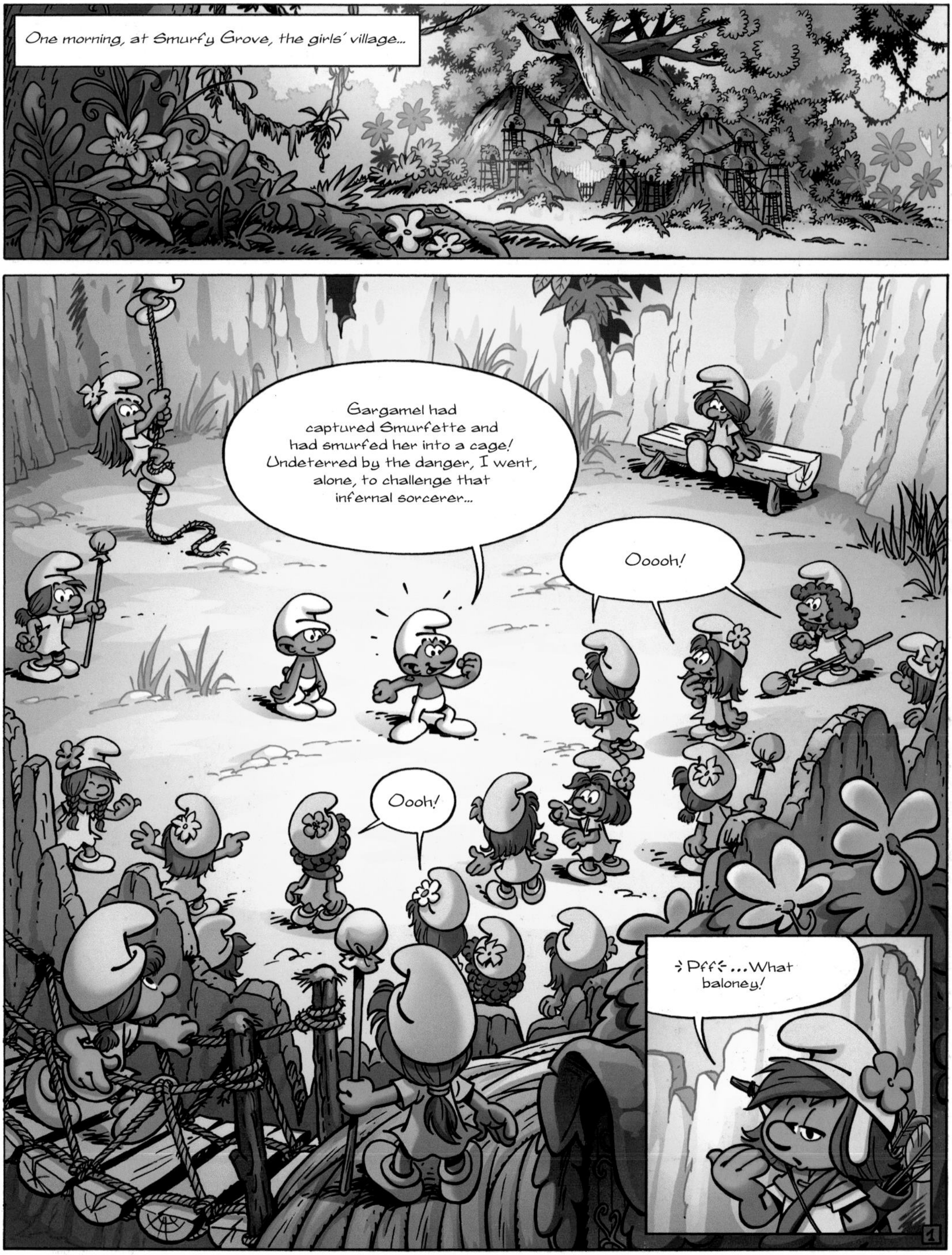

One morning, at Smurfy Grove, the girls' village...
Gargamel had captured Smurfette and had smurfed her into a cage! Undeterred by the danger, I went, alone, to challenge that infernal sorcerer...
Ooooh!
Oooh!
Pff... What baloney!
1

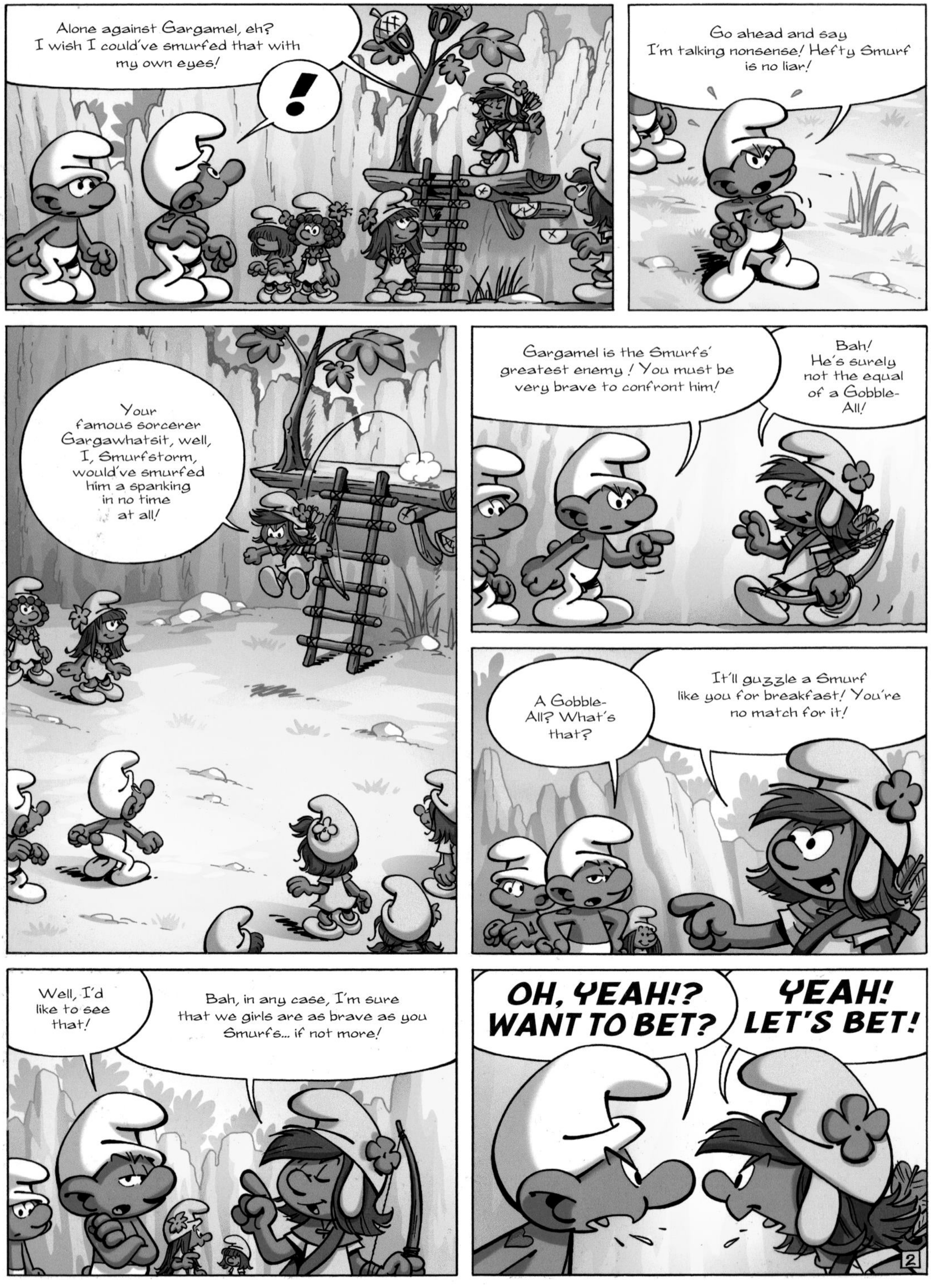
Alone against Gargamel, eh? I wish I could've smurfed that with my own eyes!
!
Go ahead and say I'm talking nonsense! Hefty Smurf is no liar!
Your famous sorcerer Gargawhatsit, well, I, Smurfstorm, would've smurfed him a spanking in no time at all!
Gargamel is the Smurfs' greatest enemy! You must be very brave to confront him!
Bah! He's surely not the equal of a Gobble-All!
A Gobble-All? What's that?
It'll guzzle a Smurf like you for breakfast! You're no match for it!
Well, I'd like to see that!
Bah, in any case, I'm sure that we girls are as brave as you Smurfs... if not more!
OH, YEAH!? WANT TO BET?
YEAH! LET'S BET!
2

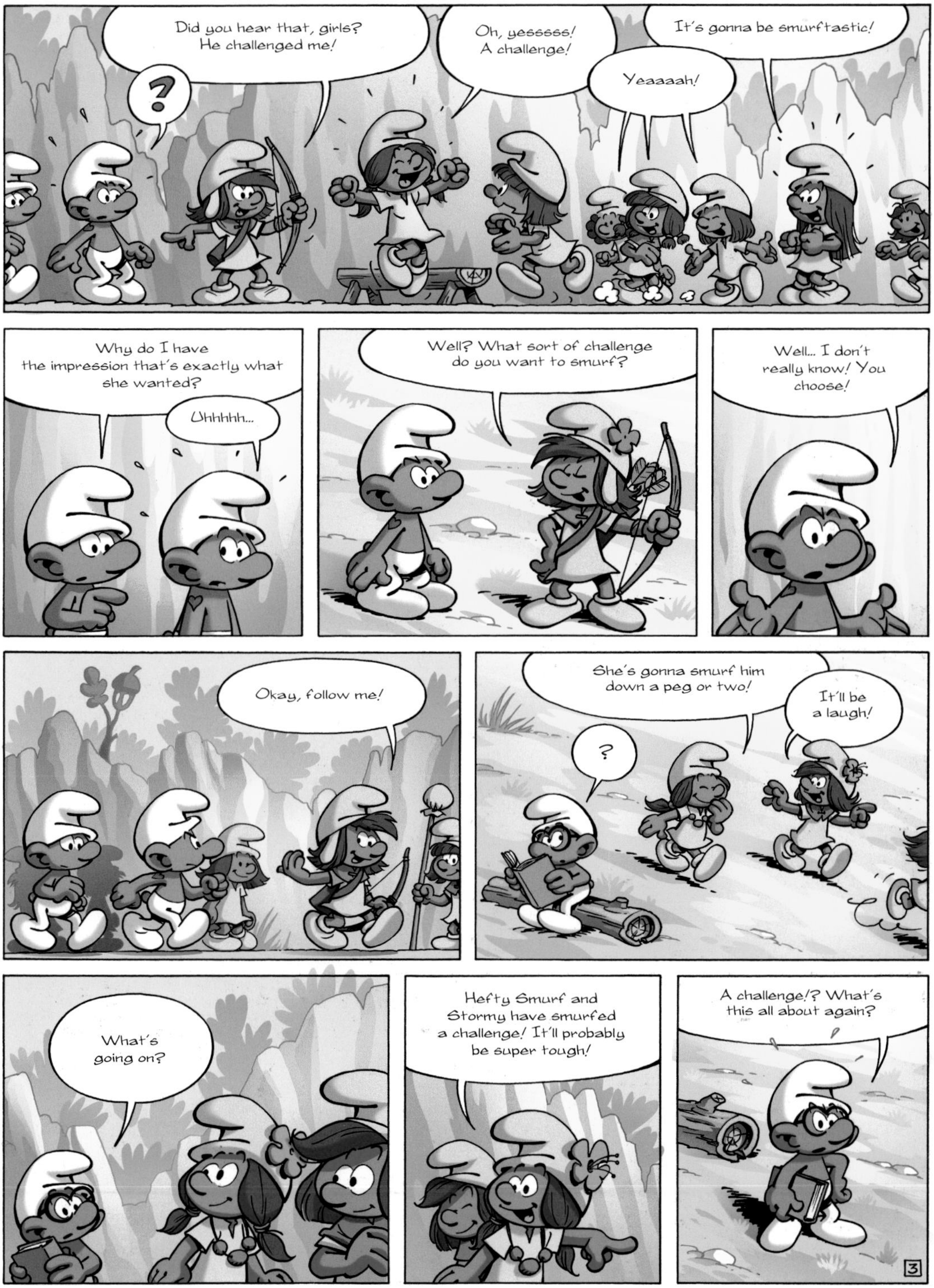
?
Did you hear that, girls? He challenged me!
Oh, yesssss! A challenge!
Yeaaaah!
It's gonna be smurftastic!
Why do I have the impression that's exactly what she wanted?
Uhhhhh...
Well? What sort of challenge do you want to smurf?
Well... I don't really know! You choose!
Okay, follow me!
?
She's gonna smurf him down a peg or two!
It'll be a laugh!
What's going on?
Hefty Smurf and Stormy have smurfed a challenge! It'll probably be super tough!
A challenge!? What's this all about again?
3

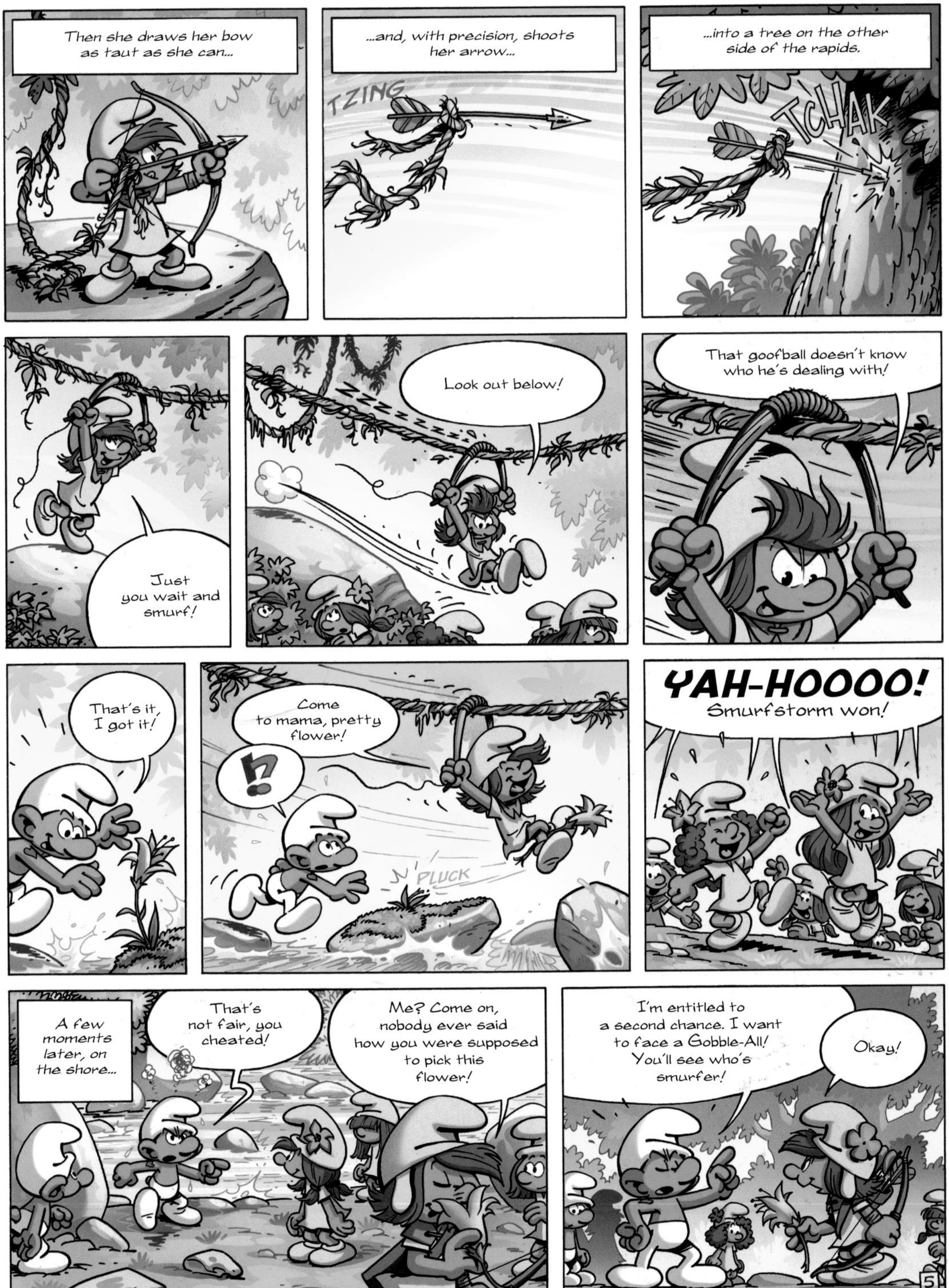

Then she draws her bow as taut as she can...
...and, with precision, shoots her arrow...
TZING
...into a tree on the other side of the rapids.
TCHAK
Just you wait and smurf!
Look out below!
That goofball doesn't know who he's dealing with!
That's it, I got it!
Come to mama, pretty flower!
!?
PLUCK
YAH-HOOOO! Smurfstorm won!
A few moments later, on the shore...
That's not fair, you cheated!
Me? Come on, nobody ever said how you were supposed to pick this flower!
I'm entitled to a second chance. I want to face a Gobble-All! You'll see who's smurfer!
Okay!
5

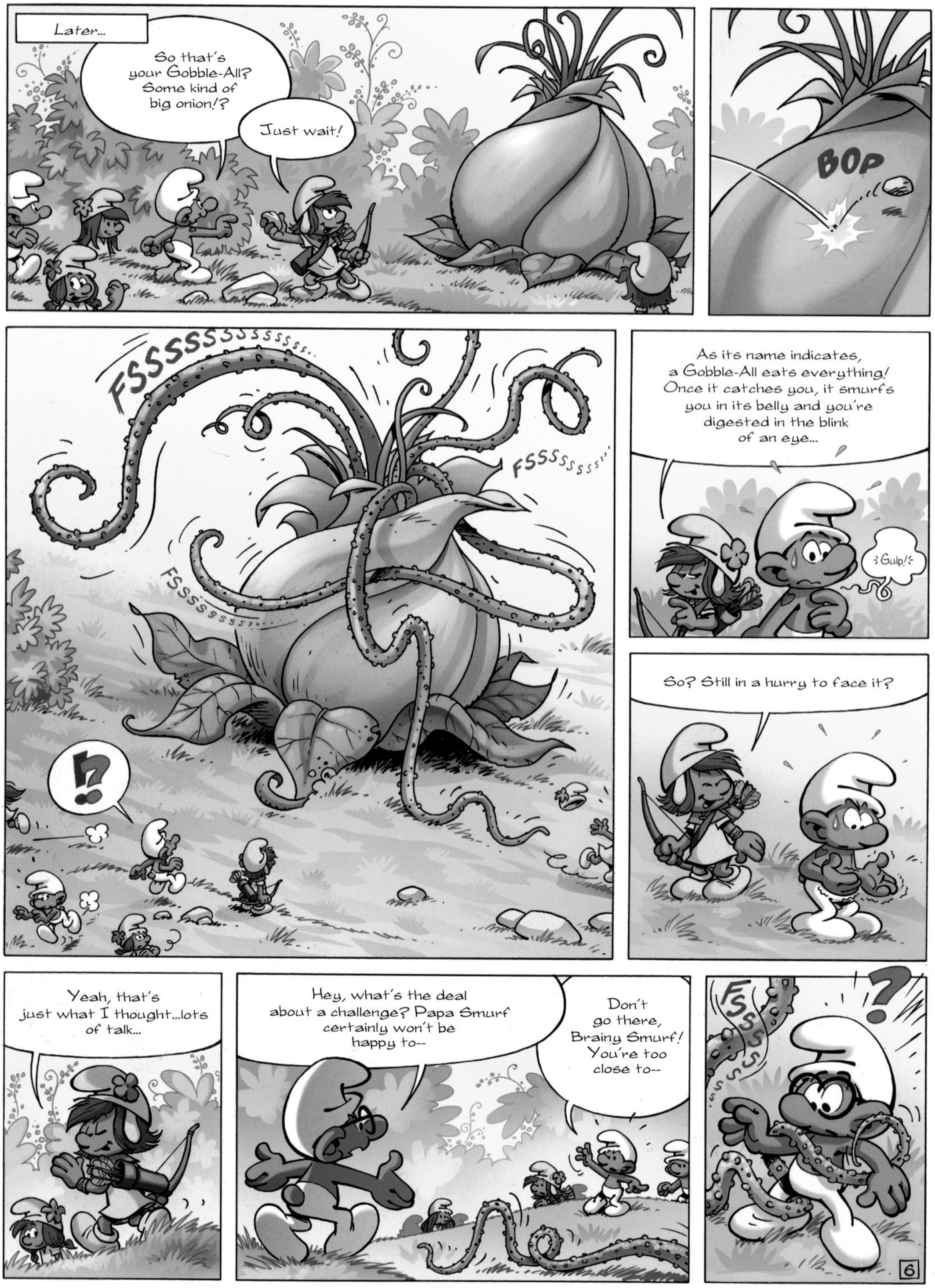
Later...
So that's your Gobble-All? Some kind of big onion!?
Just wait!
BOP
FSSSSSSSSSSSSS...
FSSSSSSSS
FSSSSSSSSS
!?
As its name indicates, a Gobble-All eats everything! Once it catches you, it smurfs you in its belly and you're digested in the blink of an eye...
Gulp!
So? Still in a hurry to face it?
Yeah, that's just what I thought...lots of talk...
Hey, what's the deal about a challenge? Papa Smurf certainly won't be happy to--
Don't go there, Brainy Smurf! You're too close to--
FSSSSS
?
6

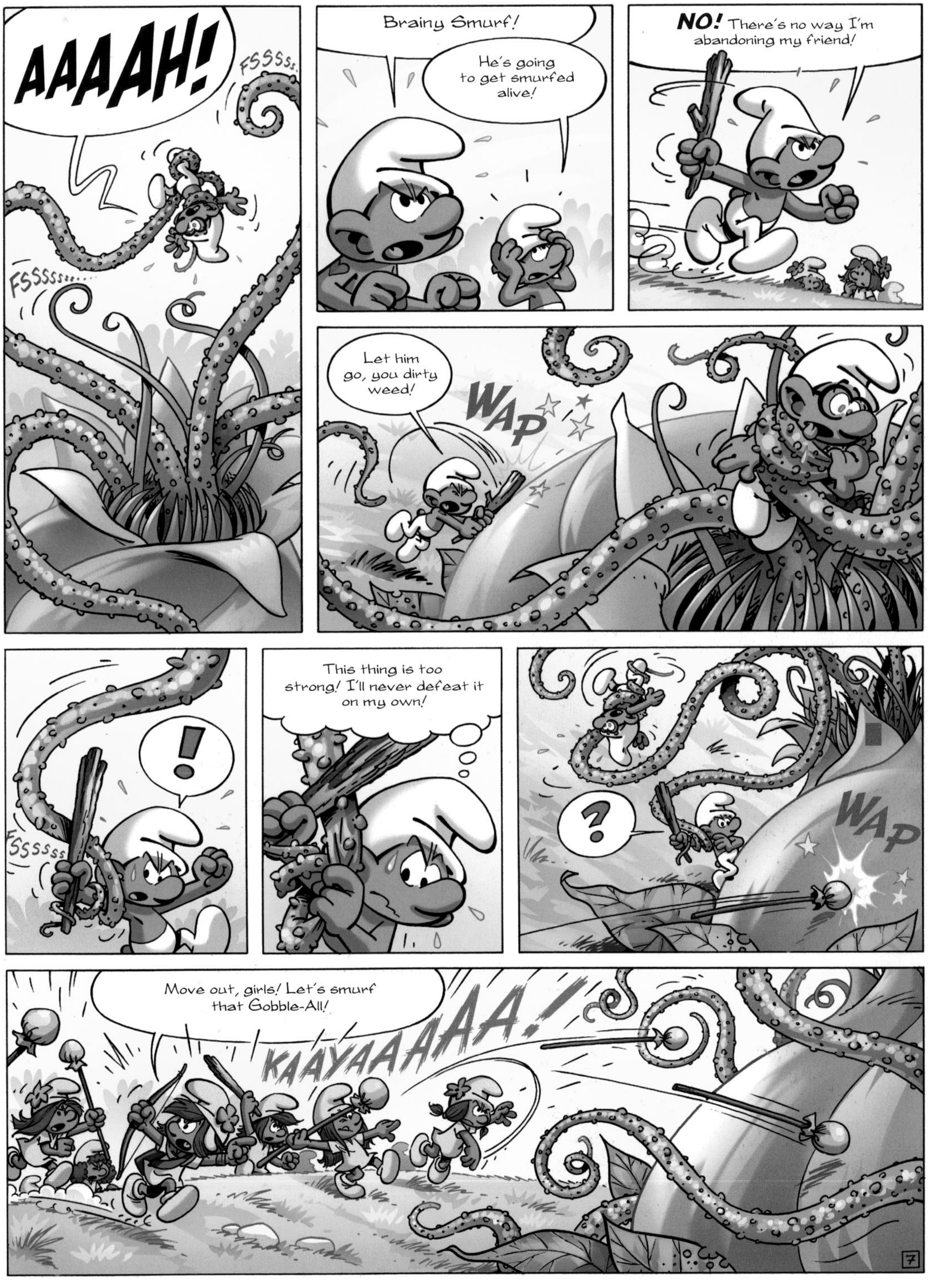

AAAAH!
FSSSss.
FSSSsss...
Brainy Smurf!
He's going to get smurfed alive!
NO! There's no way I'm abandoning my friend!
Let him go, you dirty weed!
WAP
FSSSSSS
!
This thing is too strong! I'll never defeat it on my own!
?
WAP
Move out, girls! Let's smurf that Gobble-All!
KAAYAAAAAA!
7

CLUMSY SMURF'S DRAGONFLY

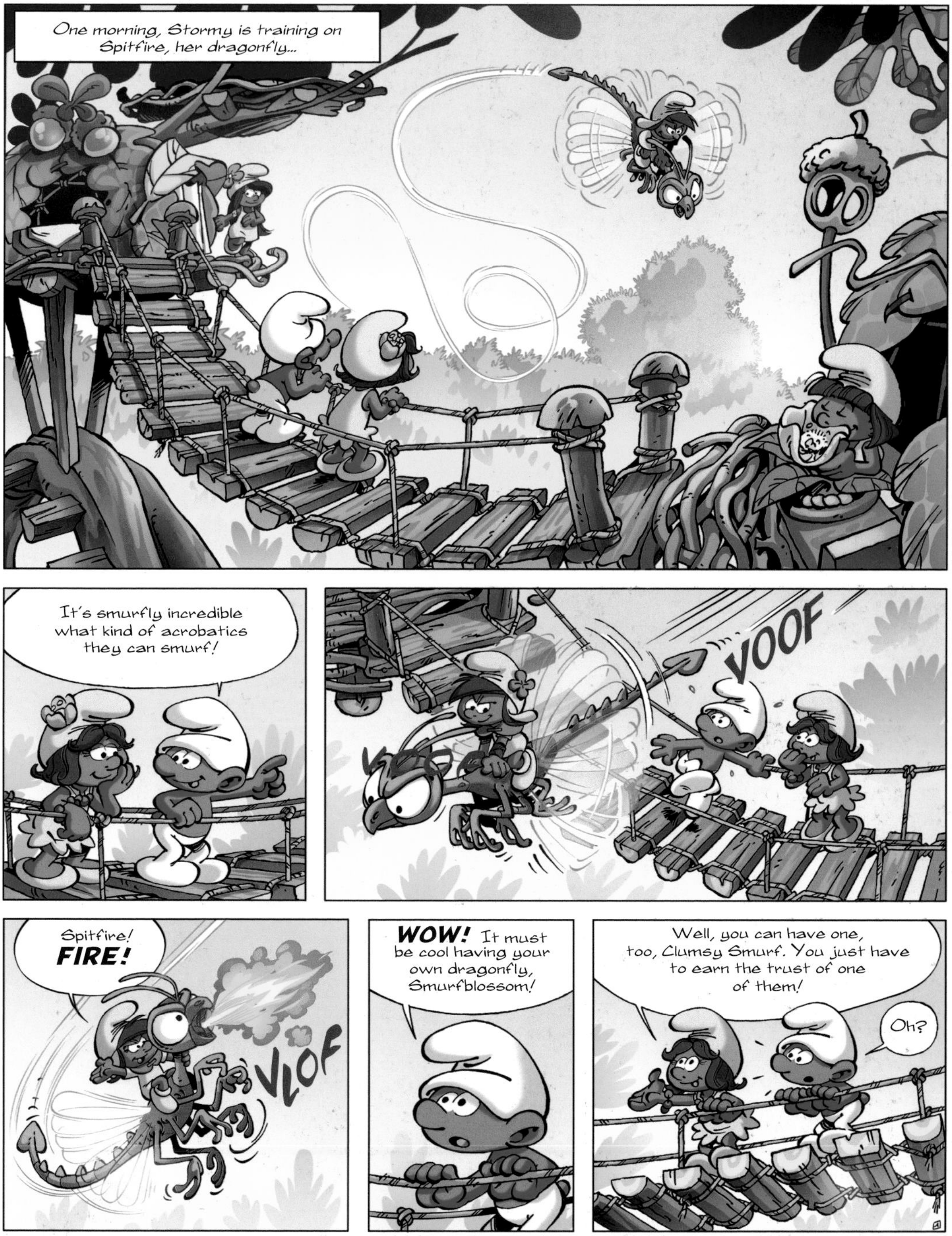

One morning, Stormy is training on Spitfire, her dragonfly...
It's smurfly incredible what kind of acrobatics they can smurf!
VOOF
Spitfire! FIRE!
VLOF
WOW! It must be cool having your own dragonfly, Smurfblossom!
Well, you can have one, too, Clumsy Smurf. You just have to earn the trust of one of them!
Oh?

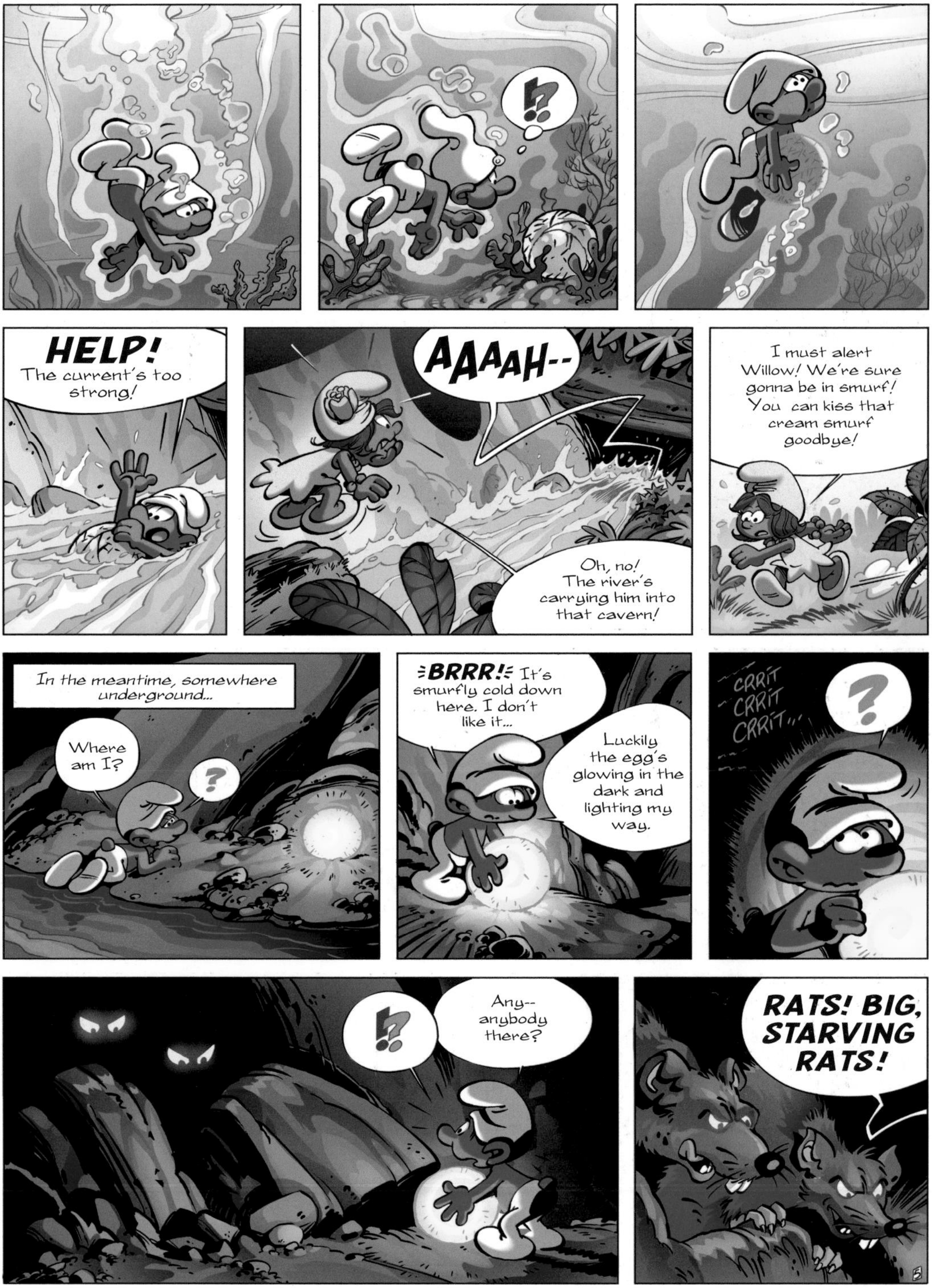

!?
HELP! The current's too strong!
AAAAH--
Oh, no! The river's carrying him into that cavern!
I must alert Willow! We're sure gonna be in smurf! You can kiss that cream smurf goodbye!
In the meantime, somewhere underground...
Where am I?
?
BRRR! It's smurfly cold down here. I don't like it...
Luckily the egg's glowing in the dark and lighting my way.
CRRIT CRRIT CRRIT...
?
!?
Any-- anybody there?
RATS! BIG, STARVING RATS!

THE SQUASH SMURFS

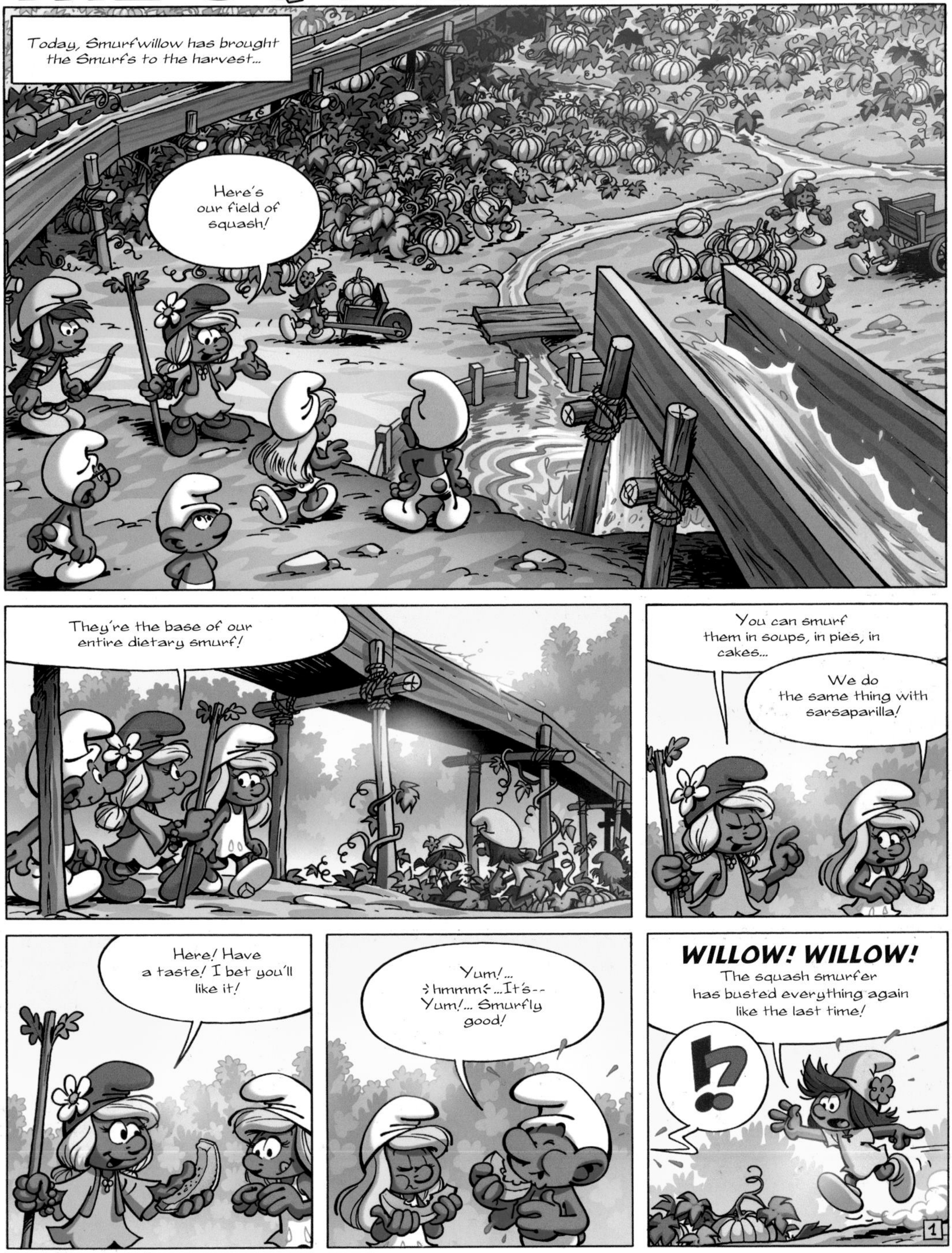

Today, Smurfwillow has brought the Smurfs to the harvest...
Here's our field of squash!
They're the base of our entire dietary smurf!
You can smurf them in soups, in pies, in cakes...
We do the same thing with sarsaparilla!
Here! Have a taste! I bet you'll like it!
Yum!... ⁖hmmm⁖...It's-- Yum!... Smurfly good!
WILLOW! WILLOW!
The squash smurfer has busted everything again like the last time!
!?
1

34

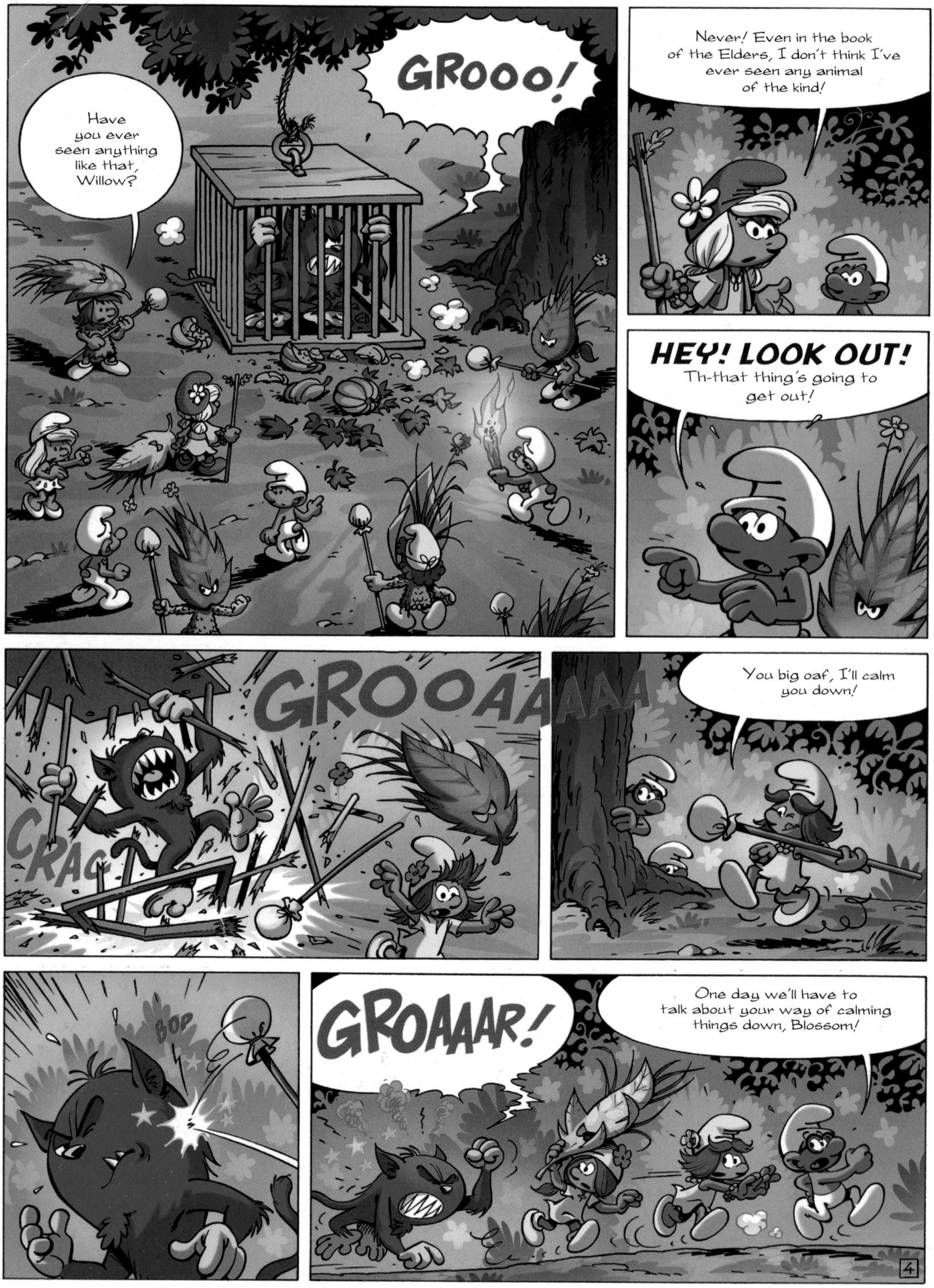
Have you ever seen anything like that, Willow?
GROOO!
Never! Even in the book of the Elders, I don't think I've ever seen any animal of the kind!
HEY! LOOK OUT!
Th-that thing's going to get out!
GROOAAAAAA
CRAC
You big oaf, I'll calm you down!
BOP
GROAAAR!
One day we'll have to talk about your way of calming things down, Blossom!
4

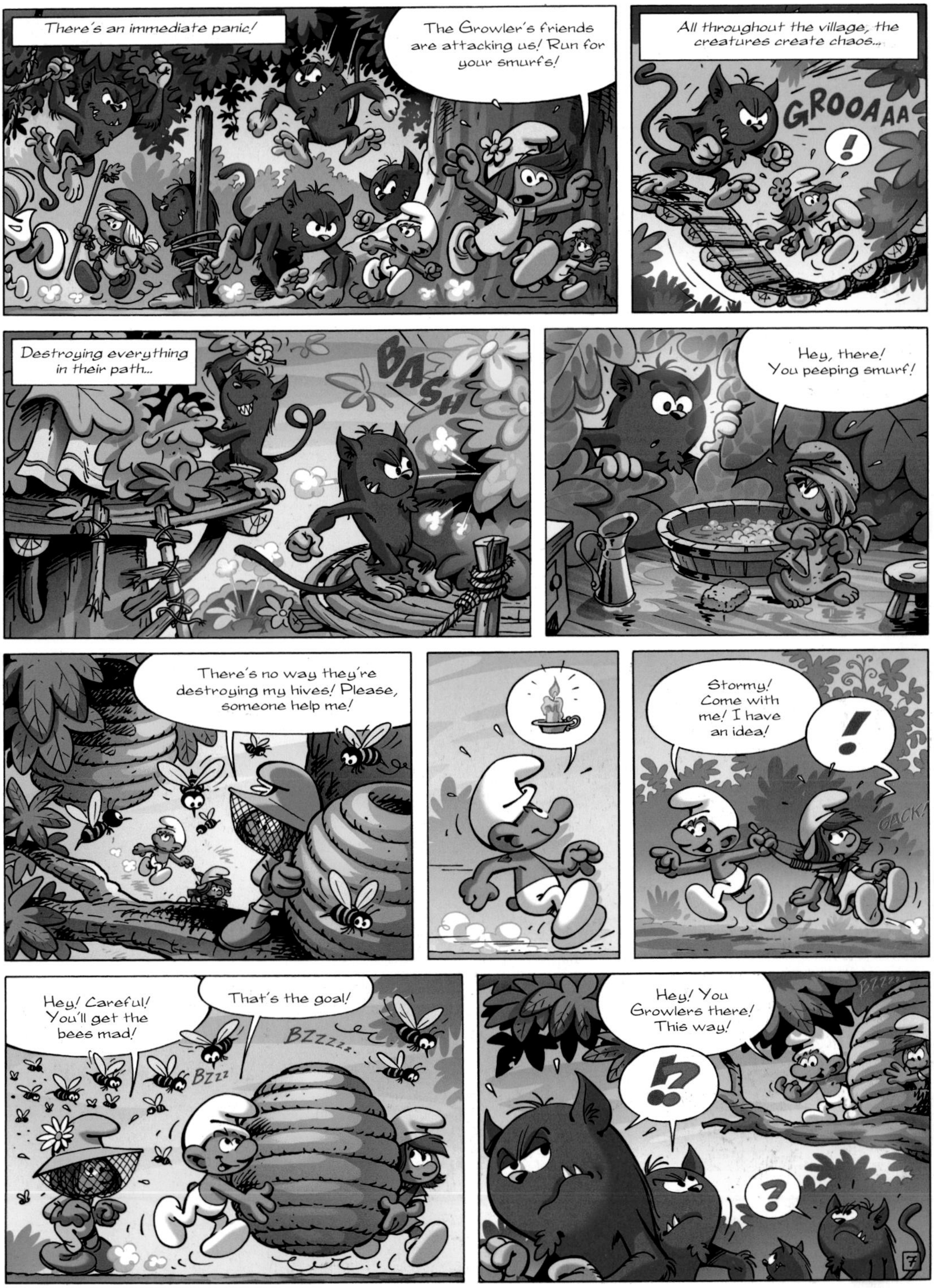
There's an immediate panic!
The Growler's friends are attacking us! Run for your smurfs!
All throughout the village, the creatures create chaos...
GROOAAA
!
Destroying everything in their path...
BASH
Hey, there! You peeping smurf!
There's no way they're destroying my hives! Please, someone help me!
Stormy! Come with me! I have an idea!
!
Hey! Careful! You'll get the bees mad!
That's the goal!
BZzzzz
Bzzz
Hey! You Growlers there! This way!
?
7

40

A SMURFLILY STRANGE WORLD

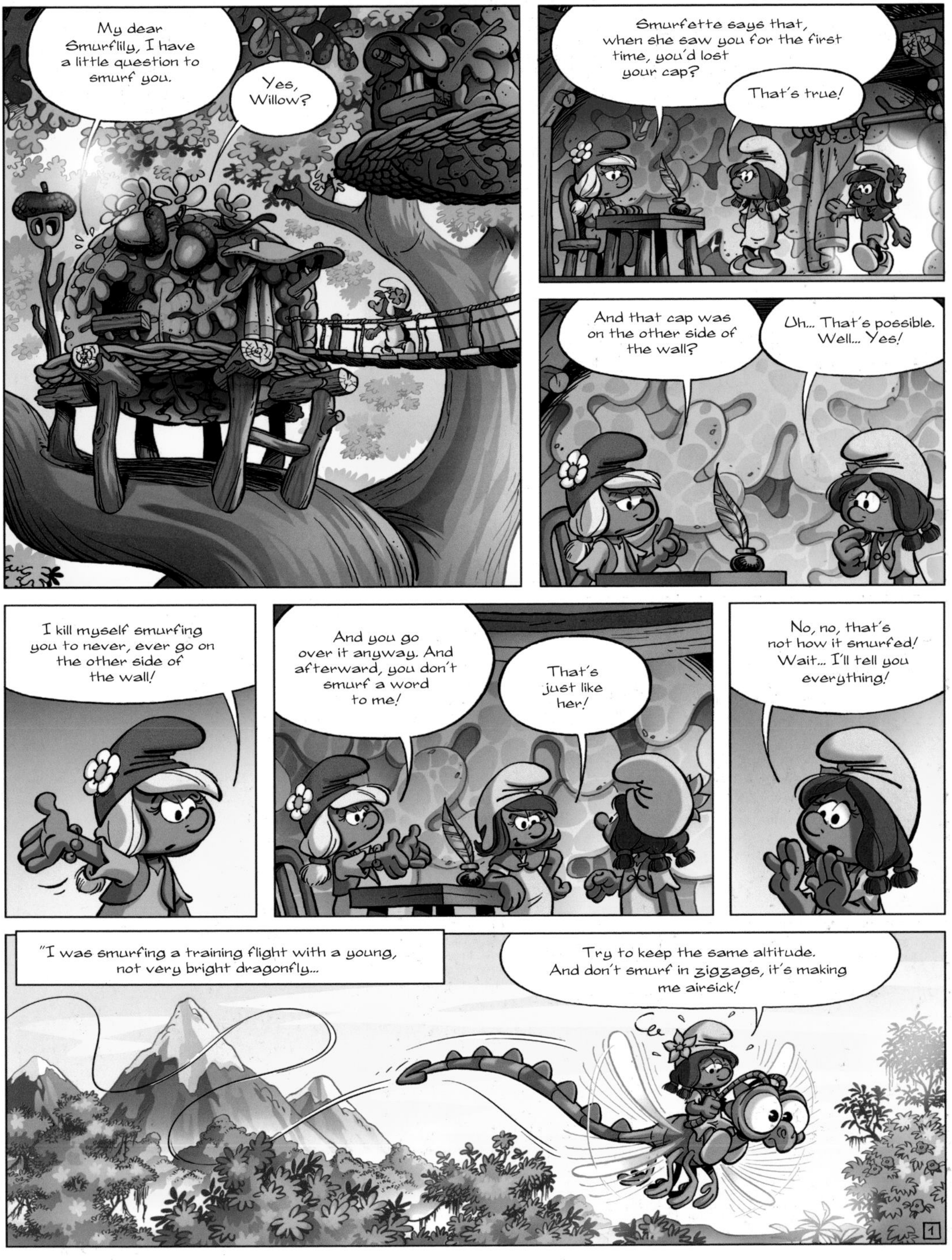

My dear Smurflily, I have a little question to smurf you.
Yes, Willow?
Smurfette says that, when she saw you for the first time, you'd lost your cap?
That's true!
And that cap was on the other side of the wall?
Uh... That's possible. Well... Yes!
I kill myself smurfing you to never, ever go on the other side of the wall!
And you go over it anyway. And afterward, you don't smurf a word to me!
That's just like her!
No, no, that's not how it smurfed! Wait... I'll tell you everything!
"I was smurfing a training flight with a young, not very bright dragonfly...
Try to keep the same altitude. And don't smurf in zigzags, it's making me airsick!
1

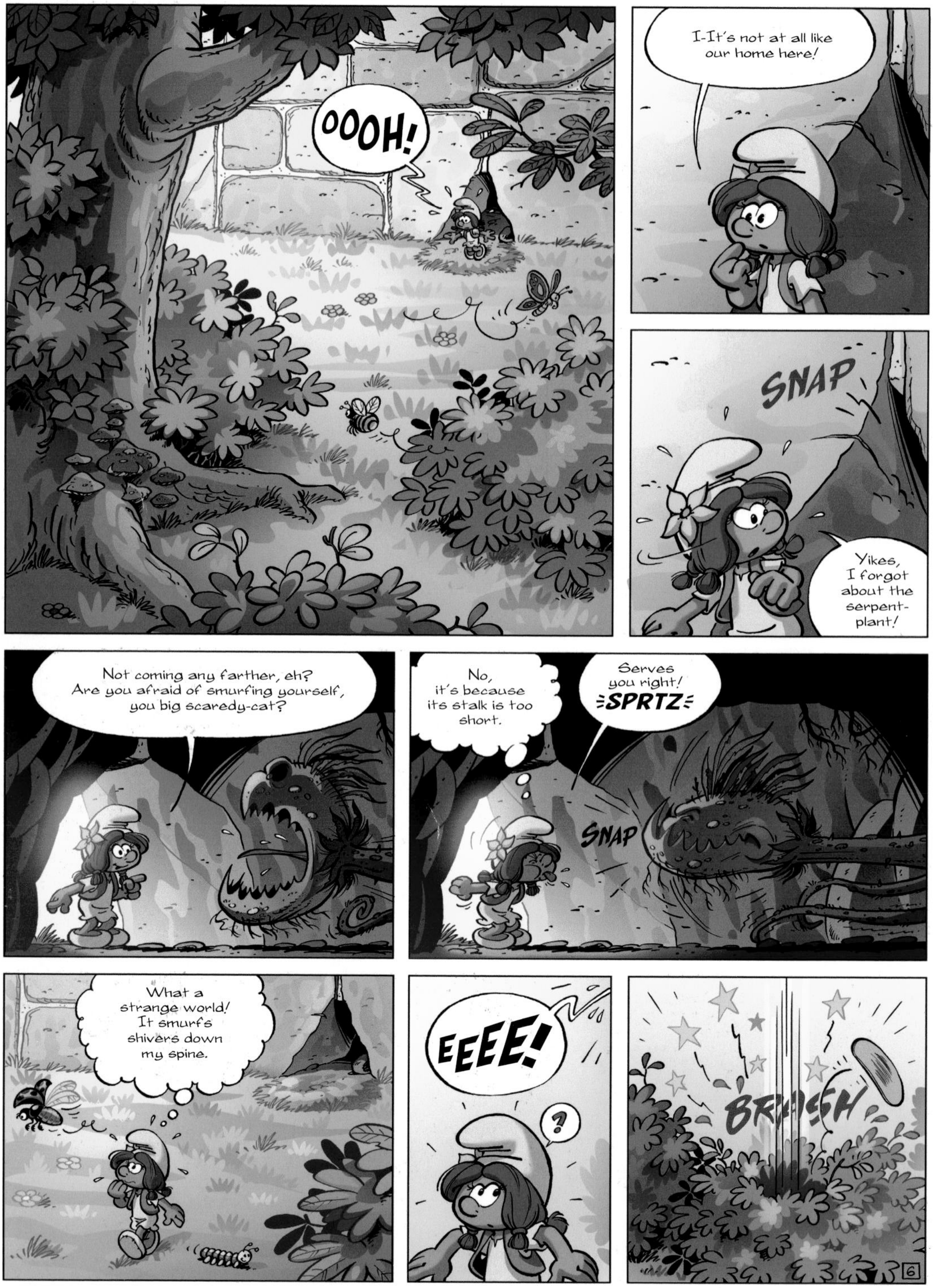
OOOH!
I-It's not at all like our home here!
SNAP
Yikes, I forgot about the serpent-plant!
Not coming any farther, eh? Are you afraid of smurfing yourself, you big scaredy-cat?
No, it's because its stalk is too short.
Serves you right! SPRTZ
SNAP
What a strange world! It smurfs shivers down my spine.
EEEE!
?
BRASH
6

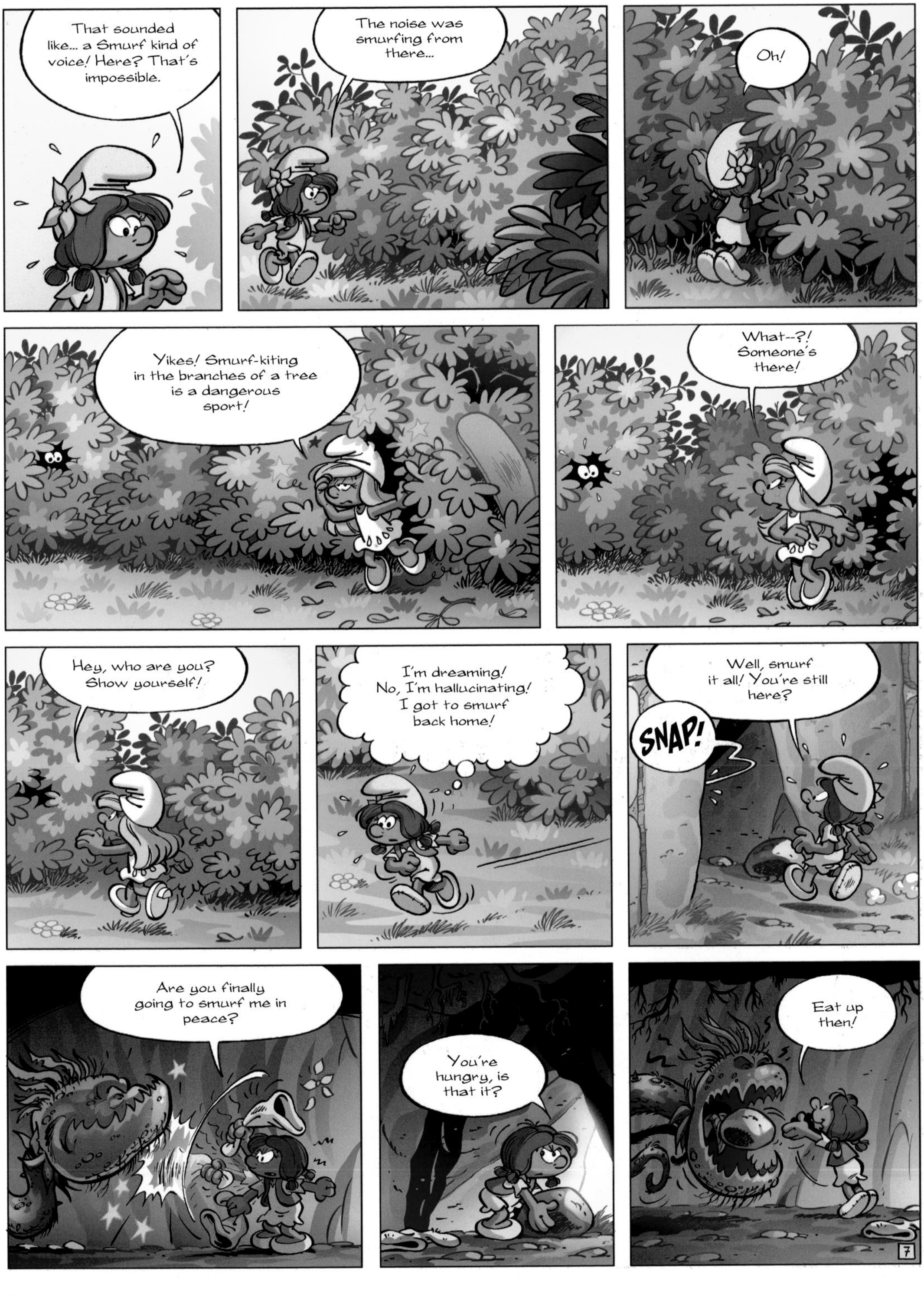
That sounded like... a Smurf kind of voice! Here? That's impossible.
The noise was smurfing from there...
Oh!
Yikes! Smurf-kiting in the branches of a tree is a dangerous sport!
What--?! Someone's there!
Hey, who are you? Show yourself!
I'm dreaming! No, I'm hallucinating! I got to smurf back home!
SNAP!
Well, smurf it all! You're still here?
Are you finally going to smurf me in peace?
You're hungry, is that it?
Eat up then!
7

WATCH OUT FOR PAPERCUTZ

Welcome to THE SMURFS "The Village Behind the Wall," the graphic novel with five all-new stories featuring the new Smurfs introduced in the *Smurfs: The Lost Village*, the hit movie from Sony Animation. I'm Jim Salicrup, the Editor-in-Chief of Papercutz, the official North American publisher of THE SMURFS comics. Papercutz is dedicated to publishing great graphic novels for all ages, and that obviously includes THE SMURFS!

While this particular graphic novel may include characters, such as Smurfwillow and Smurfstorm, who first appeared in the movie, did you know that THE SMURFS, like Batman, Teenage Mutant Ninja Turtles, Doctor Strange, and countless other movie franchises, first appeared in comics? In other words, this isn't really a comicbook tie-in to a movie or TV property, this is a comics property that has been successfully adapted in many forms of media—film, animation, video games, live shows, and more.

Sometimes comics characters change in such media adaptations, and many new characters suddenly appear as well. For example, Superman didn't really fly until he was animated in a series of cartoons produced by the Fleischer Studios, Batgirl didn't exist until she was created for the live-action Batman TV series in the late 60s, and several popular Smurfs characters, such as Puppy and Grandma Smurf, were invented for the 80s animated TV series. Likewise, the new female Smurfs made their debut in *Smurfs: The Lost Village*. But contrary to popular belief, Smurfette wasn't the only female Smurf prior to the latest *Smurfs* movie — there was the aforementioned Grandma Smurf, as well as Sassette of the Smurflings! But we're getting ahead of ourselves. While this book features the newest SMURFS comics ever published in North America, let's go back to where it all started...

In 1958, a young cartoonist, Pierre Culliford, working under the pen name Peyo (a nickname given to him by a cousin of his), was writing and drawing a light-hearted medieval adventure comic strip called *Johan et Pirlouit* (Johan and Peewit, in our English version) for the legendary Belgian comics magazine, *Spirou*. Johan was a royal page, and sort of a knight-in-training, and Peewit was the court jester. In a story entitled, *La flute à six trous*, ("The Flute with Six Holes"), our heroes, on a mission to find a magical flute, find a village of blue elves known as *les Schtroumpfs*, or, as they've become to be known in English, The Smurfs. Those minor characters, appearing on just 21 pages of a 60-page story, wound up stealing the show from Johan and Peewit, and went on to appear in a graphic novel series of their own, which continues to this day.

Interestingly, the very first time a Smurf appears in the Johan and Peewit story, it's not unlike how we were first introduced to the latest batch of Smurfs in "The Lost Village." All we see are a couple of eyes, hidden behind a few leaves. Funny how one way or another we keep going from the present to the past of THE SMURFS.

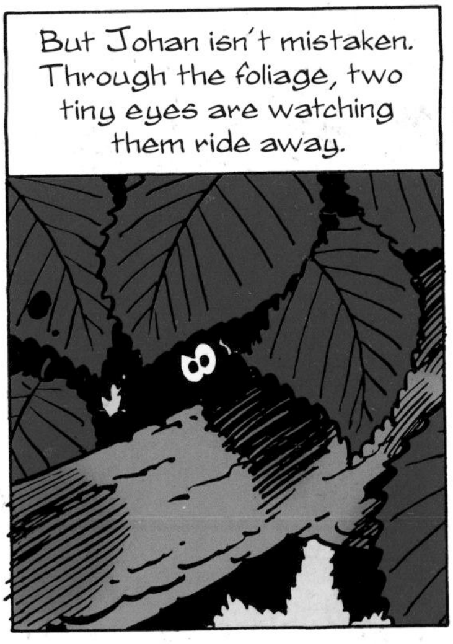
But Johan isn't mistaken. Through the foliage, two tiny eyes are watching them ride away.

A Smurf from the Village in Front of the Wall!

Cover from the French edition of this graphic novel.

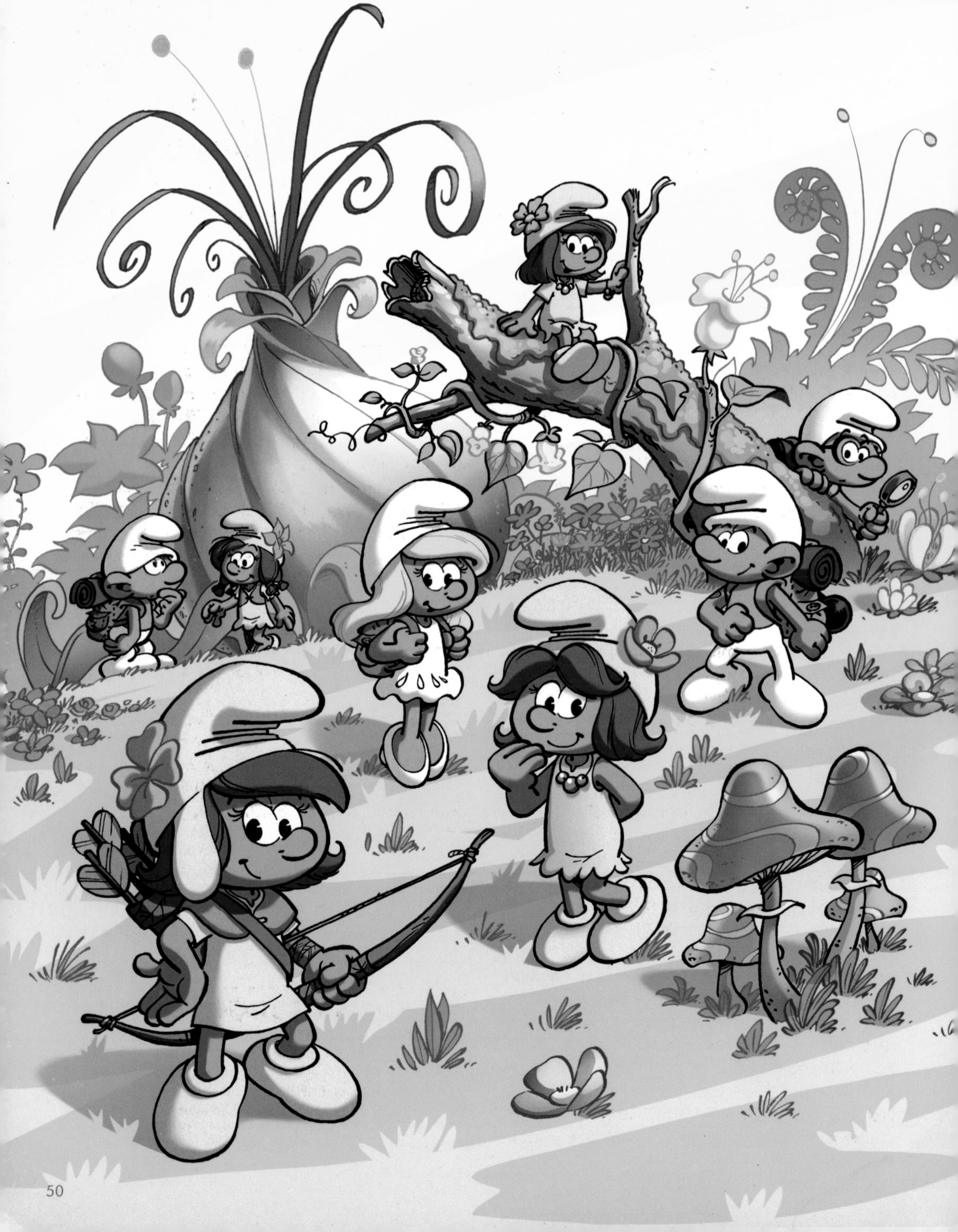

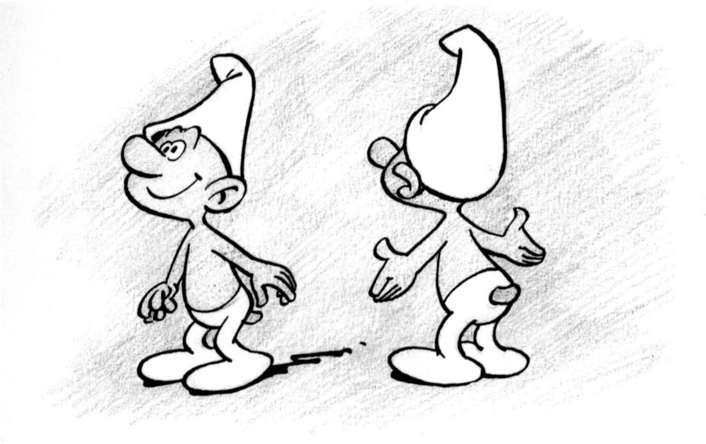

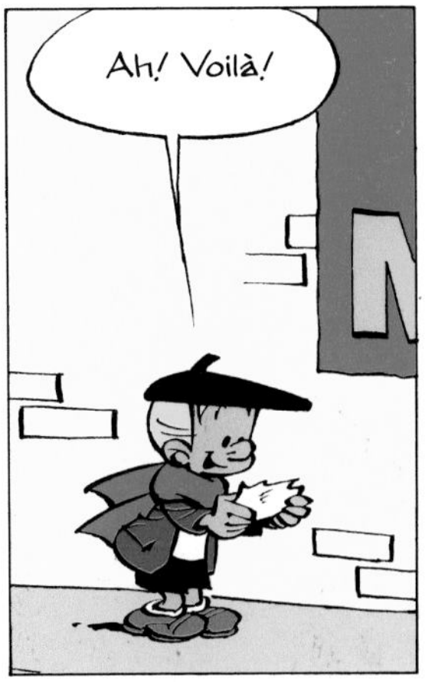
Ah! Voilà!

Left: One of Peyo's first drawings of a Smurf. Right: Benny Breakiron, recently the star of his own movie adapting "The Red Taxis."

On the following pages we offer an excerpt from that classic tale, as we see our daring duo sent to the "Cursed Land," where they encounter the Smurfs for the first time. You can get the full story either in THE SMURFS #2 "The Smurfs and the Magic Flute" or THE SMURFS ANTHOLOGY Volume One, both from Papercutz. In 2008, a prequel to that classic tale was created to celebrate the 50th anniversary of THE SMURFS, and it was published by Papercutz in THE SMURFS & FRIENDS Volume One.

Peyo, was nothing if not productive. Before he created THE SMURFS and even Johan and Peewit, he did a comic strip about a cat—a sort of precursor of Gargamel's pet Azrael—called Poussy, or as we dubbed it in English, PUSSYCAT. Much closer in style to conventional newspaper comic strips, most PUSSYCAT strips are a few panels devoted to the telling of a single gag. Yet Peyo's clear story-telling style and gentle humor is evident in every strip – from the earliest crudely drawn strips to the polished later strips drawn by the Peyo studio artists. Papercutz is devoted to publishing as much of Peyo's work as possible, in beautiful editions, and all the PUSSYCAT strips have finally been collected in one volume in English.

Inspired by the success of Superman decades earlier, Peyo put his spin on super heroes with the creation of *Benoit Brisefer*, or as we call him, Benny Breakiron. The story of a small, polite French boy with super-strength, except if he catches a cold, was set in the time period of the '60s, the first story appearing in 1960. There's a strong 60s sensibility pervading the BENNY BREAKIRON strips, with stories spoofing everything from James Bond to evil robots. Papercutz has published four volumes of BENNY BREAKIRON, and BENNY is also featured in THE SMURFS & FRIENDS.

And of course, Papercutz has been publishing THE SMURFS, both in an ongoing series of graphic novels, in large collections such as THE SMURFS ANTHOLOGY and THE SMURFS & FRIENDS, and in special editions such as this one. We're at a special time in this country, where finally great comic art is getting the respect it deserves. Bookstores and comic shop shelves are virtually overflowing with comics treasuries and omnibuses filled with great classic comics, and we're thrilled that the work of Peyo is also included on those shelves.

Unfortunately, on Christmas Eve 1992, Pierre "Peyo" Culliford passed away due to a heart attack. While Peyo may no longer be with us, his joyous spirit lives on, both in SMURFS: The Lost Village and in all THE SMURFS graphic novels.

Jim

STAY IN TOUCH!

EMAIL: Salicrup@papercutz.com
WEB: www.papercutz.com
TWITTER: @papercutzgn
FACEBOOK: PAPERCUTZGRAPHICNOVELS
SNAIL MAIL: Papercutz, 160 Broadway, Suite 700, East Wing, New York, NY 10038

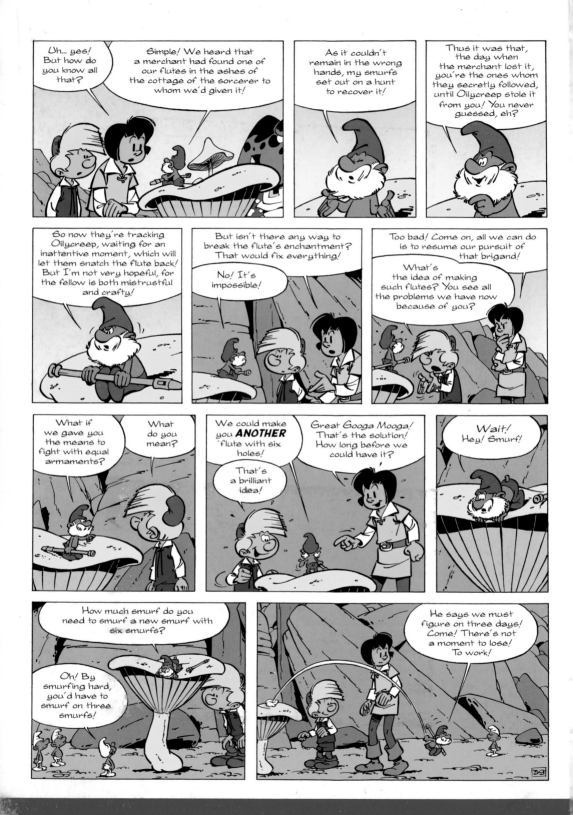

For the whole story see THE SMURFS #2 "The Smurfs and the Magic Flute" or THE SMURFS ANTHOLOGY VOL. 1